Fiction reprints published by Robert Bentley, Inc. in clothbound library editions

Nelson Algren	*The Man with the Golden Arm*
A. Anatoli	*Babi Yar*
John Brunner	*Stand on Zanzibar*
Donn Byrne	*Messer Marco Polo*
Erskine Caldwell	*Tobacco Road*
Joseph Conrad	*Almayer's Folly* *Lord Jim*
Jack Conroy	*The Disinherited*
Marcia Davenport	*East Side, West Side* *My Brother's Keeper* *The Valley of Decision*
John Dos Passos	*Manhattan Transfer*
Theodore Dreiser	*An American Tragedy* *Sister Carrie*
Daphne DuMaurier	*Frenchman's Creek* *Hungry Hill* *The Loving Spirit* *Mary Anne* *My Cousin Rachel* *The Parasites*
André Gide	*Lafcadio's Adventures* *School for Wives* *Strait is the Gate*
Nicolai V. Gogol	*The Overcoat and Other Tales* *of Good and Evil*
Ivan Goncharov	*Oblomov*
Jaroslav Hasek	*The Good Soldier Svejk*
Evan Hunter	*The Blackboard Jungle*
Christopher Isherwood	*The Berlin Stories*
Charles Jackson	*The Lost Weekend*
Shirley Jackson	*The Lottery; or,* *The Adventures of James Harris*
Sinclair Lewis	*Elmer Gantry*
Jack London	*John Barleycorn;* *or, Alcoholic Memoirs*

Frank Norris *McTeague*
The Octopus
The Pit

John Powers *The Last Catholic in America*

Jean-Paul Sartre *Nausea*

Budd Schulberg *Waterfront*
What Makes Sammy Run?

André Schwarz-Bart *The Last of the Just*

Clifford Simak *Way Station*

Upton Sinclair *Boston*
The Jungle
Oil!

Wilbur Smith *Shout at the Devil*

Josephine Tey *Brat Farrar*
The Franchise Affair
The Man in the Queue
Miss Pym Disposes

B. Traven *The Treasure of the Sierra Madre*

H. G. Wells *The Time Machine*

Sloan Wilson *The Man in the Gray Flannel Suit*

THE SCHOOL FOR WIVES

ROBERT

GENEVIÈVE

OR THE UNFINISHED CONFIDENCE

The School for Wives

※ ※

Robert

※ ※

Geneviève

or The Unfinished Confidence

By ANDRÉ GIDE

TRANSLATED FROM THE FRENCH
BY DOROTHY BUSSY

Robert Bentley
Cambridge, Massachusetts

PQ
2613
.I2
A23
1980

Library of Congress Cataloging in Publication Data

Gide, André Paul Guillaume, 1869-1951.
The school for wives; Robert; Geneviève.
Translation of L'ecole des femmes and 2 other stories.
Reprint of the 1950 ed. published by Knopf, New York.
I.   Title.
[PZ3.G3613Sd   1980]   [PQ2613.I2]   843'.9'12   79-23993
ISBN 0-8376-0454-0

CONTENTS

The School for Wives   1

Robert   95

Geneviève or *The Unfinished Confidence*   145

THE SCHOOL FOR WIVES

TO

EDMOND JALOUX

In friendly remembrance of our
conversations of 1896

1 August 1928

Sɪʀ:

After much hesitation I have decided to send you the enclosed typewritten copy of a diary left me by my mother. She died on October 12, 1916 at the hospital of X, where she had spent five months nursing contagious cases.

I have not permitted myself to change anything in it except the proper names. If you think it not impossible that these pages may be read with profit by certain young women, I give you leave to publish them. In that case I should like to entitle them *The School for Wives,* if you do not think it unbecoming to use this title after Molière's play. Needless to say, the words "Part One," "Part Two," "Epilogue" have been added by me.

Please do not try to find out who I am and allow me to sign this letter with a name that is not my own.

Gᴇɴᴇᴠɪᴇᴠᴇ D.

3

PART

i

7 October 1894

My friend,

It seems to me that it is to you that I am writing.
I have never kept a journal. I have never, indeed,
written anything at all except a few letters. And I
should no doubt write letters to you if I didn't see you
every day. But supposing I die first—I hope I shall,
for life without you would be nothing but an empty
desert—you will read these lines; I shall feel I am
leaving you less, if they remain behind with you. But
how can I think of death when all life is before us?
Ever since I have known you—that is, ever since I
have loved you—life has seemed so beautiful, so useful, so precious, that I want not to lose any of it; I
mean to preserve every crumb of my happiness in this
book. And what else should I do every day after you
have left me but recall your presence and live over
again the moments that have gone by all too quickly?
Before I met you it made me unhappy, as I have told
you, to feel that my life was without an object. Nothing could be vainer, it seemed to me, than all those
society occupations which my parents encouraged
and which constitute my girl friends' whole pleasure.
A life with no unselfish purpose in it could not satisfy

5

me. You know I once had serious thoughts of becoming a nurse or a little sister of the poor. My parents shrugged their shoulders when I spoke to them of this. They were right in thinking that all such inclinations would vanish when I met the man of my soul's choice. Why will not Papa understand and accept that you are he?

You see how badly I write. I was crying when I wrote those last words, and they seem to me frightful. Why did I read them over again? I don't know whether I shall ever learn to write well. At any rate, trying doesn't help me.

Well, I was saying that before I met you I was looking for some object in life, and now you are my object, my occupation, my very life itself, and I look for nothing more. I know that it is through you, by means of you, that I shall get what is best out of myself; that you must guide me, lead me to the beautiful, to the good, to God. And I pray to God to help me vanquish my father's opposition; and I write my fervent prayer down here, as though that might make it more efficacious: Dear Lord, do not force me to disobey Papa. You know that I love Robert and that I can belong only to him.

To speak truthfully, it was only yesterday that I began to understand what the object of my life must be. Yes, it was our conversation in the Tuileries Gardens that opened my eyes to the part woman may play in the lives of great men. I am so ignorant that unluckily I have forgotten the examples he gave me, but at any rate I brought away this—that my whole life must be henceforth devoted to enabling him to accomplish his glorious destiny. Of course, that is not what he said, because he is modest; but it is what I thought, for I am proud for him—though, in reality, I think that, in spite of his modesty, he has a very clear conception of his own worth. He has not concealed from me that he is very ambitious.

"Not for myself," he said with a charming smile, "but for the ideas I stand for."

I wish my father could have heard him. But Papa is so obstinate about Robert that he might have taken it for what he calls— No, I won't even write it down. Why can't he see that talking like that is no slur upon Robert but upon himself? The very thing I like about Robert is that he has no indulgence for himself, that he never forgets his self-respect. In comparison with him, it seems to me there is no one who knows the meaning of real dignity. If he chose he could completely crush me with it, but when we are alone, he takes great care never to let me feel it. I think he sometimes even exaggerates a little when he plays at being a child himself, so as not to make me feel too much of a schoolgirl beside him. And when yesterday I reproached him with this, he suddenly looked very grave, and putting his head down on my lap, for he was sitting at my feet, he murmured with a kind of exquisite melancholy: "The child is father of the man."

It would really be the greatest pity for so many charming sayings, sometimes so weighty, so full of meaning, to be lost. I mean to note down here as many as possible. He will feel glad to find them again later on, I am sure.

It was immediately after this that we had the idea of the journal. I don't know why I say *we*. The idea was *his*, like all good ideas. Well, we both of us agreed —that is, each of us, individually—to write what he called *"our* story." It's easy for me, for it's only through him that I exist. But I doubt whether *he* will be able to manage it, even if he has the time. And, indeed, I think it would be a bad thing for his mind to be too much occupied with me. I explained to him at length that I perfectly understood that he had his career, his thoughts, his public life, which my love must not interfere with; and that if it was right for him to be the whole of my life, I could not, ought not, to be the whole of his. I should be curious to know what of all this he has noted in his journal, but we have taken a solemn vow not to show our journals to each other.

"It is only so that they can be sincere," he said as he kissed me, not on my forehead, but exactly between the eyes, as he is fond of doing.

On the other hand, we have agreed that the one of

us who dies first is to bequeath his journal to the other.

"Of course," I said rather foolishly.

"No, no," he answered very gravely. "The promise we must make is not to destroy them."

You smiled, dear, when I said I should not know what to put in this journal. And, as a fact, I have already filled four pages. It is all I can do not to reread them; but if I reread them, it would be more than I could do not to tear them up. What surprises me is how much I am already beginning to enjoy this writing.

12 October 1894

Robert has been suddenly called away to Perpignan to see his mother, about whom he has had rather bad news.

"I hope it won't be anything," I said.

"Yes, one always says that," he answered with a grave smile, which showed how much concerned he really was. And I at once reproached myself for my absurd remark.

If all the commonplace actions I do and all the commonplace remarks I make were taken out of my life and conversation, what would remain? And to think that I had to come into contact with a superior being before I was able to realize this! What I admire about Robert is precisely that he does not say or do anything like ordinary people; and yet there is nothing affected or pretentious about him. I have been seeking for a long time the best word to describe his appearance, his dress, his talk, his behavior; "original" is too marked; "individual," "special"— no; the word "distinguished" is the one I come back to; and I wish the word had never been used for any- one else. I think he cwes the extraordinary distinction of his manners, and, indeed, of his whole personality, to himself alone, for I gather from what he says that his family is rather middle-class. He says that he is not ashamed of his parents; but this in itself shows that a nature less noble and straightforward than his *might* be ashamed of them. His father, I believe, was in business. Robert was still very young when he died. He does not seem to like speaking of him, and I am afraid to question him. I think he is very fond of his mother.

"She is the only person you would have a right to be jealous of," he said to me in the early days of our engagement. He had a sister who was younger than he and who died.

I am going to take advantage of his being away, and of the free time it leaves me, to tell here how we became acquainted with each other. Mamma wanted to drag me off to a tea at the Darblays' to hear a Hun- garian cellist who is said to play remarkably well; but I pretended I had a bad headache, so that I might be left in peace and alone—with Robert. I can't

understand how I could have been attracted so long
by "the pleasures of society"; or rather I understand
now that what I really liked about them was having
my vanity flattered. Now that the only thing I want
is Robert's approval, I don't care at all about pleas-
ing other people, or else only for his sake and because
I see what pleasure it gives him. But in those days,
so recent but which seem so long ago, how much I
valued the smiles and applause and compliments, and
even the envy and jealousy, of some of my friends
after I played the orchestra part of Beethoven's Fifth
Concerto on a second piano (rather brilliantly, I must
admit) while Rosita played the solo. I pretended to
be modest, but I was really flattered at receiving more
congratulations than she did. "It's nothing astonishing for Rosita; she's a professional; but Éveline—"
The people who applauded most were the ones who
understood nothing about music. I knew they didn't,
but all the same I was pleased with their praise, when
I ought to have laughed at it. I even thought: "After
all, they have better taste than I gave them credit
for." And so I let myself be taken in by all this absurd mummery. Yes, I see there might be a certain
amusement in making fun of it. But when I am in
company, I always seem to myself the most ridiculous person there. I know I am neither particularly
pretty nor very witty, and I can't understand what
Robert saw in me to fall in love with. The only talent
I had for making a show in society was being able to

play the piano fairly well; and now, a few days ago, I gave up playing the piano, for good no doubt. What's the use of it? Robert doesn't like music. It's his only fault that I know. But on the other hand he takes such an intelligent interest in painting that I'm surprised he doesn't paint himself. When I said this to him, he smiled and explained that when one was "afflicted" (that is the word he used) with too many different gifts, the great difficulty was not to make too much of the ones that least deserved it. If he had really taken up painting, he would have had to sacrifice too many other things, and it was not by painting, he said, that in his opinion he could be of the most service. I think he wants to go in for politics, but he did not actually say so. For that matter, whatever he undertakes, I am certain he will succeed. And it even makes me rather sad to feel that he has so little need of my help in order to succeed in anything he attempts. But he is so kind and pretends he cannot get on without me; and the thought is so sweet that I indulge in it without believing it.

I get carried away into talking about myself, which I had determined not to do. How right Father Bredel is to warn us against the snare of selfishness, which, he says, sometimes takes on the mask of sacrifice and love. One likes sacrificing oneself, for the pleasure of thinking oneself useful, and one likes hearing oneself called so. To be perfect, self-sacrifice should be known to God only and expect recognition and reward from

Him alone. But I think nothing teaches one modesty better than to love someone with great qualities. It is when I am with Robert that I realize most all the things I am lacking in; and yet of small account as I am, I long to add my little to his much. . . . But I started off to tell *our* story, and first of all, how we met.

It was six months and three days ago, on the 7th of April 1894. My parents had promised me a tour in Italy as a reward for my prize at the Conservatoire; my uncle's death, however, and the difficulty of settling up his affairs because of the children's being under age, had delayed this plan, and I had given up all hopes of it when my father suddenly took me off to spend the Easter holidays in Florence, leaving my mother in Paris to look after her small nieces. We stayed at Pension Girard, which Mme de T. was quite right in recommending to us. The boarders all happened to be of "good society," so that there was nothing unpleasant in having meals at the same table with them. Three Swedes, four Americans, two English, five Russians, and one Swiss. We were the only French people, with Robert. Every language was spoken, but especially French, because of the Russians, the Swiss, and us three, and also a Belgian, whom I had forgotten. None of the guests were disagreeable, but Robert's distinction outshone all the others. He sat opposite my father, who is rather reserved and often not very affable to people who are

not in his set. As we were the last comers, it was
natural enough for us not to take part in the conversation at once. Personally I should have liked to talk,
but I couldn't very well be more amiable than Papa;
so I copied his reserve, and as I was sitting next him,
our silence made a kind of little island of coldness
in the midst of the general animation. The amusing
thing was that we could go nowhere without meeting
the people of our pension. Papa simply had to answer
their bows and smiles, and when we sat down to
table, everyone knew that we had just come back
from Santa Croce or the Palazzo Pitti. "It's unbearable," said Papa, but all the same he began to
unfreeze. As for Robert, we met him everywhere.
When we went into a church or a picture gallery, the
first thing we saw was sure to be Robert. "Goodness!
There he is again!" cried Papa. At first Robert used
to pretend not to see us, so as not to be indiscreet;
for he was far too quick not to understand that these
continual meetings irritated Papa. So he used to
wait till Papa condescended to recognize him, and he
never bowed first but pretended to be absorbed in
the contemplation of some masterpiece. And sometimes Papa's bow was a long time coming, for it was
especially to Robert that he was so standoffish. It
was even rather embarrassing for me, for his stand-
offishness was so great that I must say it came very
near being insolence; and it required a person with
Robert's good temper not to take offense. But as I

couldn't help smiling, he understood that, at any rate on my side, there was no ill will. The colder Papa was, in fact, the harder I found it not to smile; but fortunately Papa did not notice this, for it went on rather behind his back. Robert had the good taste not to show that he saw and he never addressed me directly—a thing Papa would have taken very ill. I rather reproached myself for these little goings-on, which in a way set up a tacit understanding between Robert and me unknown to Papa. But what was there to do?

What increased Papa's coldness was that Robert's "views" were not the same as his. I have never understood very clearly what Papa's "views" are, for I know nothing about politics; but I know that Mamma reproaches him with what she calls his "materialism," and that Papa is not very fond of priests. When I was young, I used to be surprised that he was so good, for he never goes to Mass, and I think that it is not very true that "religion does not make people better," as he says. Mamma says he is "stubborn," but I think he has a better heart than she has, and when they have an argument together— which happens only too often—Mamma speaks to him in such a way that my sympathy goes to him rather than to her, even when I can't feel that he is in the right. He says he doesn't believe in heaven, but Abbé Bredel replies that he will have to believe in it when he gets there, for he will certainly go there straight away and be saved in spite of himself. That I believe with all my heart.

How sad such disputes are between couples as thoroughly united as my parents, and about points, too, on which, with a little give and take, it would be so easy to come to an understanding! In any case, there is nothing of the kind to be feared with Robert, for I have never seen him enter a church without praying, and all his ideas are generous and noble. I cannot believe that the *Libre Parole* is a "bad paper," as Papa says; he himself reads only the *Temps*, and I thought that mischief was brewing on the second day at Pension Girard when Papa and Robert happened to be sitting alone together in the smoking-room. The drawing-room door was wide open and I could see them, each in his armchair, with his newspaper in front of him. Robert, after he had looked through his, was rash enough to hand it to Papa with a few words I couldn't catch; but Papa got into such a rage that he upset his cup of coffee, which he had put on the arm of his chair, right over his light-colored trousers. Robert made a great many apologies, but it really wasn't his fault. And while Papa was wiping himself with his handkerchief, Robert, who had caught sight of me in the drawing-room, expressed his regrets by a very discreet little dumb show that he performed for my benefit, which was so comic that I couldn't help laughing; but I turned away quickly, because it looked as if I were laughing at Papa.

And then, lo and behold, on the sixth day Papa had an attack of gout. . . . Oh, it is abominable of me to be pleased at that! And of course I offered to stay in to keep him company and read to him, but the weather was very fine and he insisted on my going out. Then I made the most of his not being there, by going to the Spanish Chapel, because he is not very fond of the primitives; and of course I met Robert there and I couldn't do otherwise than speak to him. But after he had expressed his astonishment at seeing me alone and inquired politely after Papa's health, we talked of nothing but painting. I was almost glad of my ignorance, for it gave him an opportunity of explaining everything to me. He had a big book with him, but there was no need for him to open it, for he knows the names of all the old painters by heart. I could not quite succeed in sharing his predilection for the frescoes, which seem to me still very rudimentary, but I feel sure that everything he said was right, and my eyes were opened to a great many qualities I should never have appreciated by myself. And after that I let him take me off to San Marco, where I felt as if I understood painting for the first time in my life. It was so marvelous, losing oneself, forgetting oneself in a common admiration, that in front of Fra Angelico's great fresco I unconsciously took his arm, and I didn't notice I had done so until some other people came into the little chapel, where up to then we had been alone. For that matter, Robert didn't say anything that Papa mightn't have heard; but yet, when I got back to the pension, I didn't tell Papa of this meeting. It was no doubt wrong of me to hide a thing that had made such an impression on me that I could think of nothing else. But when, a little later, I confessed this sin of "lying by omission" to the Abbé, he more or less reassured me; it is true that I told him of my engagement at the same time. The Abbé knows that Papa doesn't approve of it, but he knows too that what prevents him from approving of it are Robert's opinions, and it is precisely because of his opinions that Mamma and the Abbé approve of it. And then Papa is so kind that he couldn't hold out for long. Besides, as he says, what he cares about most is that I should be happy; and he can't doubt my happiness.

Before speaking of my engagement, I ought to have told about the last days in Italy; but I let my pen run on quickly so as to get to that wonderful word which turns all my other memories pale. Before we left Florence, Robert asked Papa's leave to come and see us in Paris. I was terribly afraid Papa might refuse! But it turned out that Robert knew our de Berre cousins quite well, and they invited us to dinner with him, which made things much easier. The next day Robert came and paid his respects to Mamma, and a few days later he came again to ask for my hand. (What a stupid expression!) Mamma was a little surprised at first, and I was much more so when she told

me about it, for Robert had never really made me a
declaration. He laughed a great deal when I confessed
this, and "declared" that it hadn't occurred to him,
but that he was quite ready to make a "declaration"
if I hadn't understood that he loved me. Then he took
me in his arms, and I felt that *I* had no need to speak
either, for him to understand that I gave myself
wholly to him.

A telegram has just been brought in. I let Mamma
open it, though it was addressed to me.
"Robert's mother is dead," she said, and handed
me the telegram. I could only read one thing in it—
that he is coming back to me on Wednesday.

13 October

A letter from Robert! But it's written to Mamma,
and I think she was pleased by this mark of deference. I can see that Mamma wishes to keep the letter,
for it is a very beautiful one; and as I want to be able
to reread it, I copy it out here:

Madame,

Éveline will forgive me for writing to you today
rather than to her. I would not trouble her bright
spirit with the sight of my grief, and it is to you I
turn in my tears. Since yesterday there is no one but
you to whom I can give the dear name of Mother,
and I am sure you will let me transfer to you the

respect and tenderness I felt for her whom I have just lost.

She in whose arms I first saw the light died yesterday in mine. She lost consciousness only a few hours before the end. She still retained it in the morning while she received the last sacraments from the priest I called in. She faced death calmly and seemed to suffer only for my grief. Her last happiness, she told me, had been to hear of my engagement and to know that she was not leaving me alone in the world. Would you repeat this to Éveline and tell her that I shall never cease to regret that it was too late for Mamma to know her?

Accept, dear Mother, I beg you, the assurance of my already filial and always respectful devotion.

ROBERT D.

My poor dear, I should like to take part in your grief. I have tried to be unhappy—but I cannot. My heart is flooded with gladness, and every feeling that I share with you—even sorrow—is joy to me.

15 October

I have seen him again. How beautiful and dignified his grief is! I am beginning to understand him better. I think he has a horror of set phrases, for he talks to me of his loss with as much reserve as he first told me of his love. And he even avoids anything likely to be affecting, for fear of showing his emotion too much.

In fact, there has been no reference between us to any but practical matters; and to Mamma he has only talked of the settling up of his mother's affairs and the sale of the property that is coming to him. I find it very difficult to fix my attention on such matters, and I leave it to Mamma to go into them with Robert. I gather that we are going to be rich, and I am almost sorry for it; I should like to leave wealth to people who have need of it in order to be happy. But this is not a question of happiness. Robert tells me that he would always have enough for himself, and that he only looks upon money as a weapon with which to make his ideas triumph. He had a long talk about it with Father Bredel, who also says that one has no right to reject wealth, but that it brings with it the duty of using it for good.

Poor Papa! He is out of all this. Every time he sees Abbé Bredel come into the room, he hurries off with a sketchy little bow: "So sorry! . . . Absolutely obliged to go out." I am always afraid the Abbé may take offense; but he is so kind, so conciliatory, that he pretends to believe in these very flimsy excuses.

"Monsieur Delaborde is always so busy!" he says to Mamma, who does her best to cover up Papa's rudeness by being extra pleasant herself. And I feel that if he were only to try the least little bit, Papa would get on so well with the Abbé! For *he* is very kind and good too.

"My dear little girl, the priests and I don't worship

the same God," he answers when I try to convince him. "Don't insist; I should get cross. You will perhaps understand these things later, if you aren't too much like your mamma." Then I am simply obliged to say that I hope I shall never understand "these things," but that I must disapprove of opinions that come between my parents, both of whom I am equally fond of. It's these wretched *opinions* of his, too, that prevent him from approving of my engagement.

"My dear child," he said to me, "I don't consider I have the right to oppose your marriage, and I dislike exercising authority. But don't ask me to approve of a decision I regret. All I can do is to hope you may not soon have cause to repent it."

19 October

This morning I asked Papa what fault he found with Robert. He looked at me a long time, screwing up his lips without saying a word; then:

"I find no fault with him, my dear; I simply don't like him. If I were to tell you why, you would object, because you love him, and when one loves a person, one doesn't see him as he is."

"But it is because Robert is what he is that I love him!" I exclaimed.

"Robert has taken you all in—the Abbé and your mamma and you—himself too, I am afraid, which is more serious!"

"You mean, he doesn't believe what he says?"

"No, no; I believe he believes it. I am the one who doesn't believe it."

"But, Papa, *you* don't believe anything."

"It can't be helped, my dear. I'm what your mother calls a skeptic."

And then we stopped, for conversations like these do nothing but distress us both. Poor Papa! I count on Robert to convert him—in time. He is so patient with Papa, so yielding, so clever. He takes care to avoid everything controversial (so does Papa, for that matter). He calls talking to Papa "the egg-dance," because he has to pirouette skillfully among delicate subjects without touching them. But how I wish Papa could hear him sometimes when he talks to me, as he talks when Papa isn't there! In Papa's presence I feel he is on his guard; but as soon as he lets himself go, his whole person becomes animated and he says such wonderful things that I want to write them down at once. And then he can be so witty too, so funny. As Yvonne de Berre said the other day: "One never tires of listening to him." That was last Thursday; we had lunched with Robert at my cousins'. Maurice de Berre and Papa went out directly after lunch; then Robert talked to us for a long time about Perpignan, about the little jealousies of provincial life he is so familiar with, about the society in which he used to live and which he wouldn't go back to for a kingdom. To hear him talk of all the quaint people who made up his parents' set makes me sorry I never knew them; but of course I understand that a superior mind like Robert's must have found such surroundings stifling. He was so anxious to escape from this atmosphere that at first he thought of taking orders, for he is exceedingly pious by nature; then he realized he might do more good by mixing in active life. Abbé Bredel approves, and I agree with him that such a light ought not to be "put under a bushel," to quote Scripture like him. When one hears Robert talk, one can't help longing for other people to hear him too. This is a thing I can't be jealous about, and I feel it would be impious to keep such a treasure to myself. The object of my life must be to help him with all my might to make the most of himself.

Next week we are to pay some visits together. I am looking forward to introducing him to our friends.

26 October

I have been leading such a giddy life for the last few days! Every day I have been hoping to find a little time to write in this notebook. But it's not only time that is wanting. Even in the moments when I am alone, I can no longer find the necessary quiet of mind for thinking. I am living in a whirl—visits, shopping, dinners, theaters—to which Robert fortunately doesn't mind accompanying me in spite of his mourning, for, as he says, true feeling is quite independent of conventions; and besides, I think, in reality, the joy of feeling himself loved is stronger than his grief. He goes shopping with me and orders all sorts of things for me, which he tries to persuade me will be of the greatest use to us. It amuses him so much, and he so obviously enjoys spoiling me, that I don't attempt to stop him as much as I ought. We chose a love of a ring together, which I must confess delights me and which I never tire of admiring. But when he wanted to give me a bracelet too, I refused point-blank, in spite of what he said to try to persuade me to accept it—that buying jewels was not so much spending money as making "an investment"; that is the word he used. Then he explained to me that precious stones and metals are "certain to increase in value." I declared that it was a matter of perfect indifference to me, and then we had a little dispute. I suppose it was not very nice of me to say that I should have liked my ring as much if I hadn't known that it had cost a great deal of money; upon which he exclaimed: "You might just as well say that you prefer trash." Then, as always happens—and that's what makes him so interesting—he widened the question and looked at it "from the general point of view," which is the only one he cares about.

"People imitate pearls so well nowadays," he explained, "that anybody may be taken in; but real pearls represent a fortune, and the others have only the appearance of value."

He likes to be there when I try my dresses on, because his taste is marvelous, and a discussion with the dressmakers amuses him. We went to choose my hats together, too. I find it very difficult to get accustomed to the new shapes. Robert thinks they suit me very well, but when I look at myself in the glass, I seem unrecognizable. I think, though, that it is probably a matter of habit and that soon, as he says, it is my young girl's face that will seem strange to me. In general, I think he chooses things that are too fine, but I understand that he wants me to do him honor and that I have no longer the right to be modest. The Abbé knows that I still am in my heart of hearts, and he says that is the only thing that matters. Every day I am astonished afresh at my happiness and never cease thinking myself unworthy of it. I am afraid sometimes that Robert may find out how much he has overestimated my good qualities. But perhaps, by dint of love, I shall succeed in raising myself to his level. I hope so with all my heart and continually strive to. He helps me too with such patience.

30 October

Robert is amazing. He knows all sorts of celebrated people and has acquaintances in every kind of set. This enables him to be of great service when people ask for help; and as everyone knows how kind he is, they don't hesitate. He says that it shows great wisdom in life never to ask for anything one isn't certain of getting. But as the people he has obliged refuse him nothing, and as he only asks for things that are right, he easily gets everything he wants. All doors are open to him and I never go with him anywhere without seeing people come up to him from all sides. I have asked him to introduce me only to his real friends; but as soon as one knows him a little, it is difficult not to become his friend, and as he is so well up in every subject, he is able to talk to anybody about anything as if it were his own special line. To tell the truth, I don't think he has any intimate friends. I asked him the other day. He didn't answer in so many words, but pressing me tenderly to his heart, he said: "Friendship is the antechamber of love." And, indeed, I feel now that the great friendship I had so lately for Rosita and Yvonne was only a makeshift and that my first real friend is Robert.

He wants to surprise Papa by getting him decorated. As he knows the Minister of Education's private secretary very well, he declares it will be very easy. Papa will certainly not refuse, and in reality I think he will be very pleased. I find it very charming of Robert to think of Papa and not to ask for the decoration for himself, but he doesn't attach any importance to it and knows he can have it whenever he wants. When I hear him talking to the distinguished people he introduces me to, I realize my ignorance; I hardly dare to take part in the conversation, I am so afraid of disgracing him. I have asked him to draw me up a list of books I ought to know, and as soon as

I have a little time— But when will that be? We have decided to get married at the end of January. It seems a terribly long way off, and yet the days flash by with the most alarming rapidity. Directly after the wedding we are to go to Tunisia. It will not be merely a pleasure trip. Robert has an interest in some agricultural concern out there and he wants to look it over. He says there is no greater pleasure than one that can be turned to some advantage. His mind is never unemployed. He is always learning and manages to find profit in everything.

The great question that is occupying us is where we are to live. We have looked at a great number of apartments, but in every one either Mamma or Robert or I find some drawback. I think we are going to come to some arrangement with an architect Robert knows very well. He has just finished building an apartment house that is very well situated, in the La Muette section, with a view over some big gardens. We would be owners of the top floor, and that would enable us to arrange our rooms to suit ourselves. We spend hours together discussing plans, and nothing is more amusing. Robert, who while his mother was alive was not very well off, has contented himself during the last three years with a little ground-floor flat on the avenue d'Antin, where he was beginning to feel very cramped. He had to take his meals at the restaurant, which took up a great deal of time and was bad for his digestion. I asked to see his

diggings, which he seemed a little bit ashamed to
show me. But I was surprised to find everything so
neat. All his papers are arranged in folders or packets,
and he has invented an extraordinary system of filing
that enables him to get at any piece of information he
wants about any particular person in the smallest
possible time. That is how he is able to be of service
so easily. He considers that people as a rule are lacking in method and that society's machinery is, as he
says, out of gear. He likes quoting La Fontaine's line:
"*C'est le fonds qui manque le moins,*" and declares
that the important thing is to make the most of what
one possesses. I think this is true, especially of anyone who is as greatly gifted as he; but when I say
that *my "fonds"* is not worth much, he protests and
says very charmingly that many women who keep
salons and shine in society are less intelligent than I
am. He seems to say so in all sincerity, and I am decidedly afraid that he is full of illusions about his
future wife. May it be a long time before he loses
them! At any rate, as soon as I have a little time, I
mean to work hard at cultivating myself as much as
possible, and strive day by day to become less unworthy of him.

I was very anxious to know whether he on his side
has been able to find time to keep his journal, as we
promised each other, and I asked him to show it to
me—oh, not to give it to me to read, but just to let
me see it. To tell the truth, I was afraid he might

leave it lying about, but he reassured me; the drawer where he keeps it is always carefully locked. He showed me the drawer, but refused to take out the diary, even after I had promised not to open it.

3 November

Yesterday we had the painter Bourgweilsdorf to dine with us. In spite of his frightful name—I really don't know whether I have spelled it correctly—he is neither a German nor a Jew, but a poor, very worthy young man, whom Robert has been exceedingly kind to, and who has cluttered up the little avenue d'Antin flat with a quantity of quite unsalable pictures, which Robert buys out of charity so as to help him without wounding his pride. I told Robert that I thought it was very imprudent to encourage such a hopeless failure, and that it would be better to urge him to do anything in the world rather than paint; but it appears that the poor young man is incapable of doing anything else and, what is more, thinks he is very gifted. Robert himself, for that matter, persists in saying that he has "a certain talent," and we had a little quarrel over it, for really one has only to glance at any one of Bourgweilsdorf's horrors to see that he doesn't know his business and that he hasn't the remotest notion of what painting ought to be. Then Robert quoted a lot of painters who have become celebrated and who at first were considered mere daubers. And as he was getting a little cross, because

I couldn't sincerely succeed in thinking what he showed me was good, "You may be sure," he said peremptorily, "that if he were worthless I should not care for him." (But, all the same, Robert doesn't dare hang his frightful things—he keeps them stuffed away in a big cupboard, where I discovered them when I was poking around his flat, as he gave me leave to do.) Robert's tone was so snubbing (it was the first time he has ever spoken to me like that) that the tears came to my eyes. He noticed it and became very tender again at once, kissed me, and said:

"What do you say to making his acquaintance? You could judge for yourself then whether he is really as stupid as you think."

I agreed, and that is how we invited him to dinner.

Well! I here apologize to Robert. I thought Bourgweilsdorf almost charming. I say "almost" because all the same there is one thing about him that seems to me rather shocking—and that is his want of gratitude toward Robert. Bourgweilsdorf seems really too forgetful of what he owes him, and is actually sometimes wanting in deference. I know that it doesn't mean much, coming from him, and that the cordial way in which he said it made up for the roughness of what he said; but I heard him interrupt Robert more than once by exclaiming: "That's all rubbish, you know," after Robert had made an extremely sensible remark, to which he had not even listened. On the other hand, he approved of everything Papa said

with such courteous, smiling insincerity that it almost
took one in, and Papa, as a matter of fact, was enchanted. I expected to see a bohemian-looking person,
but he is quite a gentleman, well, not to say rather
elegantly dressed, well-groomed, and well-mannered.
He is certainly intelligent. He tells a great many
stories very amusingly, and his conversation would
be delightful if he were not rather too fond of para-
doxes. One is never quite certain that he isn't laughing
at one, as for instance when he says that Raphael and
Poussin are his two favorite painters, which one
would really never suppose from his own style of
painting. On the whole, however, it was a very pleasant evening and I shall be delighted to see our Bourg
again. But it's rather a long step from that to order-
ing him to paint my portrait, as Robert suddenly did.
Neither he nor I was expecting it, so that we didn't
know what to say and it was extremely awkward. I
must say I think Robert might have consulted me
first. I should have told him that between now and
our wedding it would be very difficult for me to find
time to sit and that we should have to put off "that
pleasure" until after we came back from our honeymoon. That's what I said to Bourgweilsdorf when, at
Robert's suggestion, he tried to fix an appointment
for the first sitting. He declared that three or four
would be enough; that he could take notes and sketch
in the portrait from memory during our absence, so
as to have only a few finishing touches to put in when

we come back. To tell the truth, when I think of his horrible daubs, I don't at all care for the idea of being painted by him. However, we have settled on a day for visiting his studio.

7 November

Shopping, parties, visits. I have no time for my diary; no time for reading, for reflection; no time for feeling myself happy. And what distresses me most is that it all tends toward making me frightfully selfish. Every day the only object in life seems to be *my* pleasure, *my* clothes, *my* convenience, *my* tastes. As if I could ever have any other pleasure or tastes than Robert's! What pleases me most, even about the furniture for my own sitting-room, is that he should choose it. He has made me a present of an exquisite little writing-table, where I shall be able to keep his letters and my journal. It is to stay in the shop until we get settled. I am longing for the time when I shall be in my own home and able to recover myself a little. This round of dissipation seems so empty—and I even feel as if I were losing sight of Robert too, as well as of myself; for though it is true that I am nearly always with him, we are hardly ever alone together; one has to be all the time in public; smiling to one and another, answering stupid questions, exhibiting one's joy, playing a kind of comedy of happiness; and such constant preoccupation with the desire of appearing happy would almost prevent me from being so, if all this show could be taken seriously for a single moment. The air of deep conviction that the most indifferent people can put on to assure me of their sympathy astonishes me; but I have to fall in with this pretense and look "delighted to make the acquaintance" of people who are perfectly insignificant or disagreeable.

12 November

I have been seeing a good deal of Yvonne lately. I feel when I am talking with her how easy it is for happiness to become selfish. What deceives me is that I think of Robert more than of myself. But when I think of him, I am only following the inclination of my heart. It is of course not a matter of loving him less, but of not confining my love to him alone. I have had eyes only for him and did not notice how ill Yvonne was looking till last Thursday. Then my eyes were suddenly opened—or rather the dazzling cloud in which I have been living cleared away; she looked so changed that I felt frightened, pressed her with questions, and at last made her confess the cause of her great trouble. She has just discovered that the young man whom I knew she loved and to whom she was practically engaged is deceiving her and is living with another woman.

"Why didn't you tell me before?" I asked.

"I was afraid of disturbing your happiness."

And then I felt ashamed of this happiness of mine.

which was like a kind of private property with a harsh "No admittance" marked up on it. No, no, I don't want a *pitiless* happiness. Yvonne has missed my friendship sadly and she is in need of help. She is afraid she will not be able to stop loving this man, though he no longer deserves her love, and she wants to find an occupation that will help her to forget her unhappiness a little. She would like to be employed in a hospital, which seems to me an excellent idea— at any rate for the moment. Of course, as I promised her, I shall keep silent about the reasons of her determination, but I shall try to enlist Robert's help. He is very attentive to Yvonne and he knows the head physician at Laënnec very well. He may recommend Yvonne with confidence, for I have no doubt that, with her devotion and intelligence and ability, she will be able to be of great service.

14 November

How kind Robert is! I had no sooner told him what Yvonne wanted than he telephoned to Dr. Marchant and made an appointment with him for dinner tomorrow evening. He has invited him to the Tour d'Argent, which is famous for its cooking. "You wouldn't believe how many things are brought off by a good dinner," he said to me, laughing. He declares that my presence will not be useless and has persuaded Papa to let me go. I am looking forward to it very much, because anything I do with Robert amuses me, and it proves that Papa is beginning to look on our marriage with a less unfavorable eye. Besides, I have hardly ever dined in a restaurant before, and if, in addition, it may do Yvonne a good turn— Robert says that Dr. Marchant is rather surly, but extremely appreciative of good food; so he means to take particular pains with the menu.

I am often afraid of vexing Robert by using certain words or expressions in my talk that he says are not correct and that I have fallen into the habit of saying because I hear them continually around me. When we are alone, Robert takes me up and corrects me. But when we are in company, I often keep silent for fear of suddenly seeing a little sign of annoyance on his face, which, though only I can notice it, makes me understand at once that I have expressed myself incorrectly. However, I must make up my mind to talk to Dr. Marchant and I tremble a little at the idea. I know myself: if I think too much about my behavior, I become self-conscious and affected. I have begged Robert not to look too much at me during the dinner. I can read in his face everything he is thinking, and the slightest shadow of disapproval I saw on it would upset me. For instance, nothing irritates him so much as the use of the word "very" before a past participle, which, as he says quite rightly, is very different from an ordinary adjective. He pointed out what I had never thought of before—that one may say "very angry," but not "very annoyed," and "very glad," but not "very pleased."

I think I grasp the shade of difference, which I confess I never dreamed of before, but now I hardly dare use the word "very" for fear of making a mistake. One hasn't always time to think whether the word that follows is a past participle or an adjective or a past participle used as an adjective. And really I think Robert pushes it a little too far. He says I may say "very tired" and yet "tired" is a past participle. He began to explain that it was *used* as an adjective, but I think he got slightly mixed himself, because he suddenly stopped his little grammar lesson and put it off till another time. I want, however, to understand these rules thoroughly and to get into the habit of applying them; for Robert considers it ought to be women's special business to maintain the purity of the language, because they are in general more conservative than men, and for them to be slovenly in their speech is to fail in one of their duties.

16 November

"My hat!" cried Papa, when he heard we had dined at the Tour d'Argent (this is his favorite little swear-word); "you certainly do yourselves well!" He told me he had never been there himself, but that he knew it was *the* gourmets' restaurant. And I had to go through all the menu in detail for him. It was

an excellent dinner and the wines were marvelous, as
far as I could judge by Robert's and our guest's
smiles as they sipped them; for personally I don't
know very much about it. But what an odious man
Dr. Marchant is!

"Idle young ladies are the very plague!" he cried
at Robert's first words about Yvonne. It was almost
at the end of dinner and when Robert thought that
our guest was sufficiently "warmed up." Then he went
on in words whose rudeness was accentuated by the
surly way in which he said them:

"Of course, she's not the first to pester me. I have
always coldly refused such offers of service. Sisters of
mercy are all very well—they have ceased to be
women, it seems. But society young ladies! Æscu-
lapius forbid! Tell your friend from me that she had
better get married. It's the best thing a woman can
do, believe me. And I'm pleased to say so before you,
mademoiselle," he added, turning to me with his
ugly smile, "as I see you think so too."

"My friend has good reasons for not doing as I do,"
I ventured to say, plucking up my courage and feeling that Yvonne's future was at stake. But my courage failed me at the jeering way in which he raised
his eyebrows and said with a sarcastic query:

"Oh, indeed?"

I was on the point of exclaiming that every woman
couldn't hope for the happiness of finding a Robert,
but I merely said in a very flat way that all marriages

were not happy. To which Dr. Marchant immediately
answered that if the married state was not always
good, the unmarried was always bad—"for women,
at any rate," he added quickly with a disagreeable
chuckle, before I had time to ask him why, in that
case, he was still a bachelor. Then, seeing, no doubt,
that he had gone too far, he went on in a more conciliatory tone:

"No, but, between ourselves, mademoiselle, is your
friend *really* so anxious to be a nurse under me?"

"I know she has always been very devoted to nursing," I began rashly; and then I felt Robert's glance
fixed upon me and realized my grammatical mistake,
so that I didn't dare finish my sentence, and Dr.
Marchant was able to go on:

"And accomplishments? What's the use of accomplishments? Why were they invented if not to give
idle young women something to do? Advise your
friend to do cross-stitch or water-colors, since she refuses to produce children, as her duty is—though
I suppose we can't very decently force her to do
it."

I no doubt showed how revolting I thought his remarks, for he very soon turned the conversation,
after having declared peremptorily:

"Besides, even if I was willing to employ your
friend, I shouldn't be able to find anything for her to
do. We are overstaffed as it is, and I can't endure
people loafing around looking at me."

So Robert has had all his expense and trouble for nothing. It's what he calls being "sold." It was easy to see by his face how much he disliked it; and I was very touched, because it was only for love of me that he took an interest in Yvonne and made these advances. I did not hide from him my opinion of Dr. Marchant. He may be a great man of science, as Robert declares, but he is an ill-mannered boor and I hope I shall never see him again, in spite of Robert's repeating: "I haven't done with him yet," as he did several times when he was seeing me home after dinner.

And it's not even as if Yvonne expected any remuneration for her services! She has enough to live on and her offer was entirely disinterested. How shall I have the heart to tell her that her offer has been rejected and that no one has any need of her devotion?

Useless! To know, to feel that one is useless! To feel that one has in one the power to help, to succor, to spread joy around one, and to be refused the means!

"You are not wanted, mademoiselle."

How dreadful! I pity Yvonne with all my heart and I am all the more grateful to God for having spared me such bitterness, and to Robert for having chosen me. But to think that so many women, less fortunate than I, are denied their share of life—to think that their right to an existence with some purpose in it, the exercise of their gifts and virtues, should be subject to some man's more or less kind permission—this enrages me. And I here register a vow that if ever I have a daughter, I will teach her none of those accomplishments which Dr. Marchant referred to so scornfully, but I will have her seriously educated, so that she may have no need of arbitrary indulgences, concessions, and favors.

I am well aware that what I have written here is absurd, but the feeling that inspired it is not. I consider it perfectly natural that in marrying Robert I should give up my independence (I have shown my independence in marrying him in spite of Papa); but every woman ought at any rate to be free to choose the slavery she prefers.

17 November

Robert is busy collecting capital to start a literary paper, of which he is to be the political editor. The paper is not to come out till we get back from Tunisia —that is to say, not till next spring; but it is well to get everything ready before we leave, which we shall do immediately after our wedding—very soon now. The care and attention he lavishes upon me do not interfere with his other activities, I am thankful to say. I should love him less if I were to be the only object of his life. I am here to help him and not to distract him from his career. It is beyond me that he must look.

19 November

Every day brings me a fresh joy. What was not my surprise this morning when Robert showed me a letter he had just received from Dr. Marchant! He seems to have forgotten—or else to be ashamed of—everything he said the other evening and asks for Yvonne to go to see him at the hospital, as he wishes to talk over with her, he says, what he can do with her, or for her.

I have not seen Yvonne again yet, and so I shall not have to tell her of my first disappointment, but only of the fortunate final result.

22 November

This morning I behaved with great weakness, but how is it possible to refuse Robert anything? I was in the little drawing-room, and as I was not expecting him to come so early, I had taken out my diary and was preparing to write an account of our evening at the Russian Ballet yesterday, when he suddenly came in and asked to see what I was writing. I answered laughingly that he would only see it after my death, in accordance with our agreement. To which he answered, laughingly too, that in that case he ran the risk of never seeing it, for in the natural course of things I should survive him; that, moreover, he had never taken our agreement seriously and that he was willing to cancel it; that, on the other hand, we had promised never to hide anything from each other; and that in any case his desire to read my journal was so strong that his whole happiness might be spoiled if I did not at once satisfy it. In short, he was so pressing, so obstinate, so tender, that I yielded, after asking that he would do the same by me, to which he willingly consented. And I left the room to let him read it at his ease.

But now the charm is broken; and that is what I feared. If I am adding these lines, it is only to explain why they are the last. Evidently it was for him that I kept my journal, but I cannot write about him any more as I used to, if only out of reserve and decency. And let him read these lines too—I do not wish to hide them from him.

No, I do not love him less; but henceforth he will know it only directly. (This sentence is perhaps nonsense, but it came from my pen naturally.)

23 November

Alas! I must add yet another postscript.

Robert has just made me very unhappy. This is the first grief he has occasioned me and I am very sorry to write it down here, as I had hoped that this book would contain nothing but expressions of my joy. But I must write it down here all the same; and I hope he will read what I am now writing, for when just now I said it to him, he would not take my words seriously.

I went to see him this morning, thinking that he in his turn would show me his journal, as he promised me yesterday before I gave him mine to read. And now he confesses his journal does not exist, that he never wrote a line of it, that he only allowed me to think he was writing it for so long in order to encourage me to go on with mine. He confessed all this, laughing, and was astonished and then annoyed because I did not laugh too and was not amused by his trick. And when, on the contrary, I was unhappy about it and reproached him—not, indeed, with not having kept a journal, for I understand that he had no time nor any desire to do so—but for letting me think he was keeping it, for duping me—he then began to reproach *me* for taking offense, for exaggerating a thing that is of no importance in itself, without understanding that what makes me unhappy is just that a thing that has so much importance for me has so little for him, and that he can treat so lightly what he sees touches me so deeply.

And soon it will not be he who was in the wrong for not keeping his word, but I who am in the wrong for objecting to it. And yet it is no pleasure to me to be in the right rather than he; I should be glad to think that he was in the right; but, at any rate, I should have wished him to show some regret for having caused me so much pain.

I feel I am ungrateful to complain like this and I beg his pardon. But I must decidedly now stop my journal here, for there is really no longer any object in it.

PART

ii

TWENTY YEARS AFTER

Arcachon, 2 July 1914

I brought this notebook away with me as one brings a piece of needlework—to serve as an occupation during the idle hours of a cure. But if I am beginning to write in it again, it is no longer, alas, for Robert. He believes from now on he knows all I am capable of feeling and thinking. I shall write to help me put my thoughts in order a little, to help me see clear in my own mind and, like Corneille's Émilie, to consider

"Et ce que je hasarde et ce que je poursuis"—
"both what I hazard and what I pursue."

When I was young, I could see nothing in this line but mere redundancy; it seemed to me ridiculous, as things often seem that one fails to understand; as the same line seemed ridiculous and redundant to my son and daughter when I made them learn the speech by heart. No doubt we must have had some experience in order to understand that we can only hope to attain in life the things we *pursue* by *risking* what may be very dear to us. What I am now pursuing is my deliverance; what I risk is the world's and my two children's esteem. The world's esteem, I try to persuade myself, I do not care about. My children's esteem is dearer to me than anything else; and as I write, I feel more deeply than ever how dear it is. I even wonder whether it is not especially for them that I am writing; if later on they happen to read these lines, I should like them to find a justification, or at any rate an explanation, of my conduct in them; for they will no doubt be taught to judge me with severity—to condemn me.

Yes, I know, I repeat it to myself continually, that by leaving Robert I shall put myself, to all appearance, entirely in the wrong. I know nothing of the law, but I am afraid that my refusal to continue living under the same roof with him may entail the forfeiture of my maternal rights. I hope the lawyer I mean to consult on my return to Paris may enable me to avoid this; it would be intolerable. I cannot consent to give up my children. But neither can I consent to go on living with Robert. The only way by which I can escape hating him is never to see him any more. Oh! above all, never to hear him talk any more. . . . As I write this, I feel that I hate him already; and in spite of the odiousness of these words, I think it was the need to write them that made me open this book again. For this is a thing I can say to no one. I remember the time when Yvonne shrank from talking to me for fear of casting a shade over my happiness. It is now my turn to be silent. And, for that matter, would she understand me? . . . It is more likely her husband would—the man I judged at first as selfish and vulgar, and whom I now know to have so warm a heart. I have sometimes detected in this really superior man an indescribable contempt for Robert; I remember, for instance, an occasion when Robert was repeating a conversation he had had, in which, of course, he gave himself the *beau rôle*, and after quoting his own words in his self-complacent way, added:

"I thought that was what I ought to say to him."

"And what did he think he ought to answer you?" asked Dr. Marchant.

Robert looked for a moment slightly dashed. He feels that Marchant sizes him up and he finds it extremely unpleasant. I think it is for my sake that Marchant refrains from openly deriding him; for I have sometimes known him exceedingly caustic to certain persons whose conceit drove him irresistibly to crush them. He is certainly no dupe to Robert's high-sounding sentences. It has even occurred to me more than once that if it were not for his affection for me, he would have given up frequenting him long ago. And that evening I felt a kind of relief at feeling I was not the only one to be exasperated by the habit Robert has fallen into of always saying "he thinks he ought" to do what he simply does because he wants to do it, or rather, still more often, because it seems to him opportune to do it. Lately he has improved even upon this; he now says: "I consider it my duty to . . ." as if he never acted except from the highest moral considerations. He has a way of talking of duty which is enough to make me take a loathing to all "duties," a way of making use of religion which casts suspicion on all religion, and of playing on noble sentiments so as eternally to disgust one with them.

3 July

I had to interrupt this in order to take Gustave to the doctor's. Thank God, the result of the consultation was very reassuring. Marchant had alarmed us so that fortunately the trouble was taken in hand soon enough. The doctor here, who is attending Gustave very carefully, even declares that there will soon be no reason to fear any relapse. He thinks that at the end of the holidays Gustave will be able to go back to the *lycée*, so that this scare will not have caused any delay in his studies.

I am not very well pleased with what I wrote yesterday. I let my pen run on, I think, out of a need for recrimination that, until I have explained myself better, may appear very vain. We all have our faults, and I know that harmony cannot be maintained between a married couple without indulgence and small mutual concessions. How is it that Robert's faults have become so intolerable to me? Is it because the very thing that exasperates me today is just the very thing I formerly found so beguiling, the very thing that charmed me and that seemed worthy of the highest praise? Oh! I must needs admit it: it is not he who

has changed; it is I. The judgments that I form today
are different. So that even my happiest memories are
marred. Ah, from what a heaven I have fallen! In
order to understand the change that has come over
me, I have reread what I wrote in this book twenty
years ago. It is with the greatest difficulty I am able
to recognize myself in the candid, confiding little
simpleton of a girl I then was! I can still hear those
remarks of Robert's that I quoted, which filled me
with such joy and love and pride, but I now interpret
them differently. I try to retrace the history of that
distrust from which I am now suffering. I think it
began on a certain day, not long after our marriage,
when my father was exclaiming over the perfection
of Robert's system of filing and asked him whether
he had found it himself, and Robert answered in an
indefinable tone, which was at once superior and
modest, profound and detached:

"Yes—I found it by dint of searching."

Oh! it was hardly anything, and at the moment I
attached no importance to it. But as I knew that this
improved system of filing came out of a stationer's
shop in the rue du Bac, where I had just been to pay a
bill, it did perhaps occur to me that there was no need
for the inspired, the almost agonized look, the in-
ventor's look, that he "thought he ought to put on,"
when he said: "I found it." Yes, yes, I know, my
dear, you found it in the rue du Bac; why say "by
dint of searching"? Or then you should have added:

"searching for envelopes in a stationer's shop." It flashed upon me then that a man of science, after making a real discovery, would never think of saying: "I found it by searching," for that would be a simple matter of course; and I saw that those words in Robert's mouth served only to dissemble the fact that he had invented nothing himself. My poor dear papa was perfectly blind to all this, and as for me, everything I have just written only became clear to me later on. I simply felt instinctively there was something indefinable that rang false. For that matter, Robert did not say the words with any intention of deceiving Papa. The little sentence escaped him unconsciously; but that is just what made it so self-revealing. It was not Papa he was taking in, it was himself.

For Robert is no hypocrite. He imagines that he really has the sentiments that he expresses. And I think even that in the long run he actually does have them, that they come at his call—the finest, the most generous, the most noble, always exactly those that it is proper—those that it is advantageous—to have.

I doubt whether many people are taken in by them; but they behave as if they were. A kind of convention is established; and it is not perhaps so much that people are really duped as that they pretend to be duped for convenience' sake. Papa, who first of all seemed clear-sighted enough at the very time when I was most dazzled, and whose opinion of Robert dis-

tressed me so much during my engagement, now seems
to have completely come round to him. In every one
of my disagreements with Robert he always takes
sides against me. He is so good-hearted, so weak;
Robert so clever! As for Mamma . . . There are
days when I feel terribly lonely; I can only say what
I think in this notebook, and I have begun to be attached to it as to a discreet, docile friend to whom I
can at last confide my most secret and most painful
thoughts.

Robert thinks he knows me; he does not suspect
that I may have a life of my own, apart from him. He
no longer considers me as anything but a dependent
of his. I form part of his comfort. I am his wife.

5 July

Whenever anyone new appears on the scene, I feel,
I know, that Robert's first concern is to find out how
to get round him—how to get hold of him. Even in
those of his acts which are apparently the most generous and in which he shows himself the most oblig-
ing to other people, I feel at the back of his mind the
desire to lay other people under obligation. And how
naïve he is about it! How natural! In the early days,
before he had learned to be suspicious of me, remarks
would escape him of the most telltale nature: "I have
a very poor reward for my kindly feelings"—as if
kindly feelings should expect a reward from others!
And I used to shudder when I heard him say:

". . . After what I have done for so-and-so, he can refuse me nothing."

This was the whole aim and object of the review that Robert edited for four years, and that he gave up only last year, after his red ribbon had been changed into a rosette. Under an appearance of impartiality, it was merely a kind of mutual aid and benefit society. Every complimentary article was considered by Robert as a letter of credit. He is extraordinarily clever too at making out that he is doing people a service when in reality he is making use of them. What would the few articles he contributed to the review have been like without that young secretary of his who put them on their feet, rewrote them, rethought them? But when he speaks of that charming, discreet, remarkably gifted, exquisitely mannered young man, I have heard him exclaim: "What would that fellow be if it hadn't been for me?"

To listen to Robert, the review's only object was to help on artists of unrecognized talent, to make them known, to "impose them on the public," as he phrased it; but at the same time it also helped him to push himself. Yes, no doubt Robert did a great deal to bring Bourgweilsdorf's extraordinary talent to light—Bourgweilsdorf, who combined so much pride with such exquisite modesty, and so sincerely despised the favor of the public. But the astonishing increase in the value of his pictures, due to the campaign so adroitly organized by the review after Bourgweilsdorf's death, enabled Robert to sell two canvases of what he calls his "gallery" for a great deal more than he paid for all the others together. They have all now been taken out of their cupboards, where he kept them for so long, and paraded on the walls, so that Robert can sententiously say to his son: "It is rare indeed that God in the long run fails to recompense us."

Ah, how I wish I could see him, if only for once, defend a cause for which he would really have to compromise himself, experience sentiments from which he could derive no advantage, have convictions that would be of no benefit to him!

When he invited Papa and our de Berre cousins and even the dear and simple-hearted Bourgweilsdorf, who was still so badly off, to invest money in the printing company, which afterward failed so miserably, it seemed as though he were doing them a great favor; "the shares were very much sought after; he could only dispose of a limited number, which as a special favor he could let his friends profit by." All that was so cleverly presented that I myself came to think: "How kind Robert is!" For I did not then understand that all this stock which he got his friends to take assured him a majority and swelled his importance immeasurably.

And after the failure what fine phrases he found to excuse himself in his own eyes for the heavy losses that his imprudence had brought on them!

"My poor dear friends. . . . They have had a fine reward for the confidence they put in me. Ah, I'm well punished for having wanted to help other people. It is enough to disgust one from trying to do good," and so on.

When it would have been so simple to reimburse without more ado Bourgweilsdorf at any rate, who had risked his money in this affair because of Robert's insistence and Robert's guarantee. As for Robert, *he* managed to get out of it with the minimum of loss, having "liquidated his situation," as he admitted to me later on, in the nick of time; and when he saw me inclined to be indignant that he had not first thought of protecting his friends' money, he gave me a confused explanation of how it was impossible to sell their shares without a power of attorney, which he had not had time to ask them for, and that, moreover, the sudden sale of too great a number of shares might have created a scare and made their values fall. I think I never despised him so thoroughly as that day; but I took care not to let him see it, and he could not suspect it, for everything he had said appeared so natural to him that he was unable to imagine that anyone in similar circumstances would not have acted exactly as he did.

6 July

I think it was Marchant who first made me realize that Gustave was like his father. All the illusions I so long nourished regarding Robert I continued till a few months ago to have about Gustave, so difficult is it for us to judge a creature we love. As I fell out of love with Robert, I imagined I had become exceedingly perspicacious, and when I transferred my thoughts and hopes to Gustave, I began by saying to myself: "He at any rate . . ." For Robert's faults reappear in Gustave, but recast, so to speak; they manifest themselves differently. But now I recognize them. Though under a new aspect, they are the same; it is impossible to mistake them. And even certain traits of Robert's character are now made clear to me through observing them in his son. I do not like to see him at school neglecting everything in his studies that he is not afraid of being actually questioned about. He never learns anything out of the simple desire to learn and cares less about knowing a thing than about giving the impression he knows it. I have had great difficulty in checking a habit he had when he was very little of constantly asking apropos of everything: "What use is it?"—which I at first set down to a charming curiosity. True, now he does not say it, but I would rather he did, for I know he is thinking it just the same and that he despises everything that is of no *use*.

And to think that at first, simpleton that I was, I congratulated myself on his choice of companions! "Gustave will only make friends with the best boys," I said to Yvonne, and Marchant smiled. Last year, when I gave a children's party, at Gustave's request and by Robert's advice, we had a cabinet minister's son, a senator's nephew, a young count—in short, not a single child whose parents were not either exceptionally wealthy, powerful, or well known. Robert himself could not have chosen better. Gustave has indeed one other friend—a boy who has taken a scholarship. His parents are teachers; they are poor. Gustave gave me to understand that it would not be suitable to invite him with the others. At first I tried to imagine it was out of tactfulness. Now I think that Gustave was simply afraid his friend would put him to shame. He likes seeing him; but it is in order to dazzle him, to show his superiority. As for me, I prefer him to any of the others; he is the only one who seems to me to have any real personal value. He is a warm-hearted boy and adores Gustave, and when I see him in admiration over his friend's sayings and doings, I feel inclined to warn him, to say: "My poor boy, don't deceive yourself. It's your devotion Gustave is fond of, not you."

"But, Mamma, it is such a pleasure to him to do things for me," Gustave answers when I reproach him for making his friend do something that he might easily have done for himself. "It amuses him, and it bores me." So that finally it is the other boy who thanks him.

9 July

The pleasure I take in covering the white pages of this book seems a very vain one, but it cannot be denied. And yet I let my pen carry me away less than formerly; I do not precisely take trouble to write well; but as I reflect more, it seems to me I write better. The best instruction I ever received was trying to instruct Gustave and Geneviève. In order to help them better to understand the authors they had to study at school, I tried first of all to understand them better myself, which is the reason that my tastes have greatly changed and that many modern books that formerly interested me I now find empty and insipid, while others, which I at first read as a task and in which I found nothing but tediousness, have grown to be full of life and light. The great writers of the past, in whom at first I saw nothing but fine language and frigid pomposity, have now allowed me to enter their intimacy so that I have made some among them my secret counselors, my friends, and often it is with them that I seek refuge, to them that I go to be cheered and consoled, as I sometimes have great need to be, for I feel terribly lonely.

11 July

Old Abbé Bredel, whom a family bereavement summoned to Bordeaux, came yesterday to spend the latter part of the day with me. He knows me so well;

in the old days I got on so well with him! . . . I confided my troubles to him, a thing I had not done for many a long day, for I have very much neglected my religious duties for a long time past. Robert's show of practicing his disaffected my heart, so to speak; the exhibition of his piety has made me doubt the sincerity of mine. His ostentatious genuflexions stop the prayer in my heart. . . . But yesterday weakness, the sickness of solitude, the need of sympathy, drove me irresistibly to talk to the Abbé, who always taught me to look on him more as a friend than as a priest. But at the end of our interview I felt beaten down, bewildered, discouraged, with as little confidence left in myself as in Robert.

The Abbé began by saying that it is not always the case that "out of the abundance of the heart the mouth speaketh"; and, as in prayer the outward act often precedes the inward grace, I ought to accept the fact that with Robert the expression of a feeling is not always accompanied by the real feeling, and to hope that it shortly—that it eventually—would be. The important thing, according to the Abbé, is not that one should say what one thinks (for one often thinks what is wrong), but what one ought to think; for in the most natural way possible and almost in spite of oneself one ends by thinking what one has said. In short, he violently defended Robert, denied me all right to doubt his sincerity, and refused to see in my grief and what he called my "selfish complaints" anything but a manifestation of the most deplorable pride—a pride that the neglect of my religious duties had fostered and developed. And gradually—so great is the empire the Abbé has assumed over me—I ceased to see clearly what it was I was complaining of, or to understand what I was reproaching Robert with; I was nothing but a recalcitrant, recriminating child. I protested through my sobs that I felt none of the rebelliousness that he saw in me, only a deep desire to serve and to devote myself, but to devote myself to something real, and that Robert's specious outside hid nothing but a great emptiness.

"Well," said he gravely and in a voice that had grown suddenly softer, "in that case, my child, your duty is to help him hide that emptiness—from all eyes," he added more gravely still, "and especially from your children's. It is of the utmost importance that they should continue to respect, to honor, their father. It is for you to help them by covering, hiding, and palliating his deficiencies. Yes, that is your duty as a Christian wife and mother; a duty you cannot shirk without impiety."

Half prostrated at his feet, I hid in my hands my sobs, my flushed cheeks, my confusion. When I raised my head, I saw tears in his eyes and felt in his heart a deep and sincere pity, which suddenly touched me more than his words had done. I said nothing, could find nothing to say; but he well understood that I had submitted.

I have been very near tearing up today all that I have written during the last few days; but no, I want to be able to reread it, if only to make me feel ashamed.

12 July

So, then, all that remains for me to do is to place myself at the service of a being for whom I have neither love nor esteem left; a being who will feel no gratitude for a sacrifice he is incapable of understanding and will not even notice; a being of whose mediocrity I have become aware too late; a lay figure whose wife I am. That is my object, my lot, my *raison d'être;* and I have no other horizon left on earth.

It was in vain that the Abbé pointed out the beauty of renouncement. "In the eyes of God," he said. And in my distress I suddenly realized that I had ceased to believe in God at the same time that I ceased to believe in Robert. The very idea of seeing him again beyond the grave, as the wretched recompense of my fidelity, fills me with horror—a horror so great that my soul refuses the thought of eternal life. And if I am not more terrified by death, it is because I feel that I do not believe in immortality, that I no longer believe in it. Yesterday I spoke of submission; but it is not true; I feel nothing but despair, revolt, indignation. "Pride," said the Abbé. . . . Very well; yes. I believe I am worth more than Robert; and the moment that I humble myself most before him will be the very moment when I shall be most conscious of my worth and feel the proudest. Does not the Abbé, who warns me against the sin of pride, understand that on the contrary he is driving me into it and that the only motive to which he can appeal to evoke humility in me is pride?

Pride! Humility! I have repeated these words so often that I have ceased to understand them, as if my conversation with the Abbé had emptied them of all meaning. And there rises in me a thought, which I repulse in vain, which has been torturing me since yesterday, and which discredits in my mind both the Abbé and everything he has been trying to convince me of—the thought that in reality the Church and he care only for the outside of things. The Abbé is very much better pleased with a sham that is of service to him than with my sincerity, which disturbs and irks him. Robert has managed to gain him over, as he manages to nab—frightful word—everybody. Praise for him—reprobation for me. Little he cares whether there is anything or not beneath the outward act. The outward act is enough for the Abbé. The outward act is enough for everyone; and it is I who am foolish to refuse to content myself with it. What I seek for beyond it has no importance, no existence, no reality.

Very well! Since it seems we must be satisfied with appearances, I will put on the appearance of humility, without feeling any real humility in my heart.

But this evening, in my distress, I should like to believe in God in order to ask Him if it is really that which He desires.

13 July

A terrifying telegram has just come from my father suddenly summoning me to Paris. Robert has had an auto accident—*"not serious,"* the telegram says, but yet I am wanted back. If Robert's state were very serious, my father would ask for Gustave to go back as well. This is what I say to reassure myself.

I am feeling frightful remorse for what I have written here during the last few days. Fortunately Gustave is well enough for me to be able to leave him alone for a few days without anxiety. The proprietor of the pension promises to look after him, and the doctor, who was here at the moment I received the telegram, has undertaken to send me a daily bulletin of his health. I am going back therefore by the first train.

Paris, 14 July

Thank God, Robert is alive. Dr. Marchant and the surgeon declare there is no need for anxiety. But how can I help taking this accident as a warning from Heaven, as Abbé Bredel, whom I found at Robert's bedside, said to me at once? The wheel of the car that knocked him down, and which might have run over him, by some miracle only passed over his left arm, causing a double fracture of the humerus, very easy to reduce, says Marchant.

What alarmed me most when I saw Robert was a bandage that hid part of his face. But Marchant says there are only a few insignificant contusions there. Robert, however, is suffering from violent pains in the head, which he bears with really admirable courage and resignation. After all I have already written here, I must add that I was very anxious about what he would say to me or rather about the irritation I was afraid I might feel. But at his first words I felt I had not ceased to love him.

"I beg your pardon for all the trouble I am giving everyone," he said simply. And as I bent over him, "No, don't kiss me; I am too ugly," he added, smiling in spite of his sufferings.

I fell on my knees at the foot of the bed, weeping, and silently thanked God for not having heard my impious complaints, for having preserved Robert to me, for having refused me the criminal liberty that I am ashamed of having desired, for which I beg God's forgiveness with all my heart.

I should feel more profoundly that God is putting my constancy to the test in this way if the Abbé did not try to convince me of it. It is his words now that arouse my antagonism, at the very same time that elsewhere I am making submission; it is as though the spirit of rebellion, which I so imprudently harbor and which I now cast from me, had fallen back on this meager prize. I leave it this bone to gnaw. But I understand today how right the Abbé was to accuse me of pride in my recent rebellious temper; how much pride there indeed is in the mean irritation I feel at hearing him preach to me a duty that I have accepted and that he has no longer any need to harp upon. I accuse myself of that too, O Lord, and I will humble myself to the point of taking example by Robert, whose merits I have misjudged.

Mamma has offered to look after Gustave for me and is leaving for Arcachon this evening.

16 July

Robert continues to complain of violent pains in the head; but the X-ray that was taken yesterday has completely reassured Marchant, who at first feared a fracture of the skull. As for his arm, he declares it is merely a matter of patience; in a month Robert will have recovered the use of it. I am reassured too; but, alas, why should anxiety have been necessary to bend me and to draw me near to Robert or call from him accents that find an echo in my heart? I think he was afraid of dying, and no doubt it was that fear that, for the first time in his life, drew from him a genuine reaction. But now that he no longer really has that apprehension, he acts it and invents sublime "last, dying words." And now that I no longer have any anxiety about him, I observe all this coldly.

The sound of his own voice moves him to tears, and

we should all be driven to shed them, too, if we did not know for certain that he was out of danger. He is too sharp, however, not to understand that with some of us his efforts are useless, so that he varies his effects in proportion to the amount of credit he feels he possesses. He hardly tries it on at all with Marchant, with whom he adopts the humorous attitude of an *"esprit fort";* he reserves the pathetic line for the Abbé, who considers him "edifying," and for Papa, who considers him "antique" and goes out of the room stifling his sobs. I think he does not feel at his ease with me and is afraid of giving himself away, for he makes a great effort to be simple, which, for him, is the most unnatural thing in the world. But I am astonished to see that there is one person with whom he is even more careful—that is Geneviève. Yesterday at some of her father's words—which were not so very pompous—I saw a kind of smile hover on her lips, an ironical curl, and her eyes sought mine, though I immediately put as much severity into them as I could. We cannot prevent our children from judging us, but it is intolerable to me for Geneviève to hope to find me in agreement with her spitefulness.

17 July

Marchant cannot exactly understand Robert's state, as he continues to complain of pains in his head; in reality, I am wrong in saying he complains, but every now and then he silently contracts his features and clenches his teeth, like someone in violent pain trying to control himself; and then if he is asked whether he is in pain, he makes a sign that he is; not even by nodding his head, but by what he no doubt thinks more eloquent, simply blinking his eyelids with the look of a person in the very act of expiring. Marchant maintains there is nothing the matter with him and remains somewhat skeptical, I believe, as to the genuineness of these agonies—puzzled at any rate—and watchful. He has called a consultation with a colleague, who has discovered nothing further, and assures me there is no cause for anxiety. But I feel that Robert does not like being reassured, or, rather, he dislikes our being reassured.

"Man's science is highly precarious," he said oracularly after the doctors had gone, adding, so as to be more impressive: "And I am speaking of the most learned."

But yesterday he refused to take any food, closed his door to troublesome visitors, of whom there are a great many, and this morning asked that my mother and Gustave should be sent for to come back from Arcachon. A telegram tells us to expect them this evening.

The difficulty for him consists in avoiding expressions too well known, celebrated "last words," "clichés"; he is aware of this and I admire the art with which he avoids them. Moreover, he speaks little.

One has not got an unlimited supply of sublime and original sayings always at hand. But one of his latest inventions is to take up a highly depreciatory tone about himself. This is marvelously successful with the Abbé, who takes it for Christian humility and contrition. When Robert sees him at his bedside, "This is the moment," he murmurs, shutting his eyes, "to compare the little good one has done with all the good one might have done." Then, as we all remain silent, he goes on: "I have bestirred myself a great deal for very little"; then turning his eyes toward the Abbé: "Let us hope that God does not measure man's effort by the smallness of the results he obtains."

At this moment I pour him out a dose of some calming medicine; after which he goes on again:

"Running water is a bad mirror, but when water is still, one can see one's face in it."

Then he stops to take a breath, turns to the wall as if to avert his eyes from a sight that is too abject, and starts afresh in a louder voice and in a tone of reproach, grief, disgust, scorn, and deep desolation:

"I see in it nothing but foolishness, spite, conceit—"

The Abbé interrupts him:

"Come, come, my friend; God, who reads the secrets of all hearts, will be able to see other things as well."

As for me, alas, all I can see in it is play-acting.

18 July

Mamma came back last night with Gustave. Before receiving his son, Robert desired to make a little toilet; but he insisted on keeping on the useless bandage that covers half his forehead. Under pretense that the lamp tired his eyes, he had it placed in such a way that his face was in shadow. Papa had gone down to see my mother and Gustave in the drawing-room and to give them the very reassuring news; Geneviève stayed with me in the room, as well as Charlotte, who was putting away the toilet things. We looked as if we were preparing a *tableau vivant*. When everything was ready, Geneviève called the others in.

It would have been the natural thing for Gustave to run up to the bed and give his father a kiss; but his father didn't intend it so. He kept his eyes shut and his face had taken on such a majestic expression that Gustave stopped, petrified. Papa and Mamma followed him into the room. Robert began:

"And now come closer—for I feel very weak."

He opened one eye and saw Charlotte, who made as though to retire discreetly.

"No, no, my dear Charlotte, you aren't in the way."

After all the last words we have had lately, I was rather curious to see what more he was going to invent, but paternal affection might afford fresh themes. So, addressing himself especially to Geneviève and Gustave, who like well-trained actors had drawn close to the bed, he began:

"My children, it is your turn now to take up the torch that—"

But he was not able to finish his sentence. Geneviève, as though she could not contain herself, suddenly interrupted him, in a clear, almost playful voice:

"Why, Father, you talk as if you were getting ready to leave us. We all know you are nearly well and that you will be able to get up in a few days. You see Charlotte is the only person you have succeeded in making cry. Anyone coming into the room would think she was the only person who had any heart."

"Master Gustave can see that his papa is crying too," exclaimed Charlotte (and in fact the tears were running down Robert's cheeks as he spoke); then, going a little nearer to the bed, and encouraged by our silence, she went on: "If you are feeling so weak, sir, perhaps it's just because you want a little something. I'll go and get you some beef tea."

After which there was nothing left for Robert to do but to inquire whether Mamma had had a good journey and whether Gustave had liked Arcachon.

P A R T

...

iii

19 July

Geneviève does not like her father. How is it I have remained so long without perceiving this? No doubt because I have for so long given her very little attention. All my thoughts and care have been centered on Gustave, whose health is delicate. I recognize, too, that he interested me more; he is somewhat of a charmer, like his father, and I find again in him all that captivated me so in Robert before so greatly disappointing me. As for Geneviève, I thought she was absorbed in her studies and indifferent to everything else. Now I have reached the point of wondering whether I did right in encouraging her to study. I have just had a terrible conversation with her; I see now that she is the one person with whom I might come to an understanding, but at the same time I see why I do not wish to come to an understanding with her. It is because I am afraid of coming face to face in her with my own thoughts, but my own thoughts grown bolder, grown so bold that they terrify me. All the fears, all the doubts, that have sometimes tortured me have turned in her into so many brazen negations. No, no, I will not be a party to recognizing them. I cannot admit that she should speak of her

70

father with such disrespect; but when I tried to shame her, "As if you took him seriously yourself!" she flung in my face, so brutally that I felt myself blush; I was incapable of answering her, or of hiding my confusion from her. Then she immediately declared that she could not admit that marriage should confer all the prerogatives on the husband; that for her part she would never consent to submit to such a thing; she was quite determined to make the man she fell in love with her partner, her companion, and the most sensible thing would be not to marry him at all. My example was a warning; it put her on her guard; on the other hand, she could not thank me enough for having given her an education that enabled her to judge us, to live a life of her own and not bind herself to a person who might very likely be her inferior.

As she was walking excitedly up and down the room, I sat listening in extreme dejection to the cynicism of her talk. I begged her to lower her voice, fearing that her father might hear her, but she went on:

"Oh, well, let him hear us! I am quite ready to repeat to him everything I have been saying to you; you can repeat it to him yourself. Repeat it to him. Yes, yes, repeat it to him."

She seemed to have lost all control of herself. I left the room. All this took place only a few hours ago.

Yes, this took place yesterday before dinner. And Geneviève was no doubt touched at seeing the sadness that during dinner I was unable to conceal. She came to my room in the evening, and flinging herself into my arms like a child, she began to stroke my face and kiss me as she used to long ago, and so tenderly that it made me cry.

"Darling Mamma," she said, "I have made you unhappy. Don't be too cross with me; but you see I can't, I won't tell lies to you. I know you could understand me, and I understand you much better than you want me to. I must talk to you more. There are things, you see, that you have taught me to think and that you don't dare think yourself; things that you believe you still believe and that I know I don't believe at all."

I kept silent, not daring to ask her what things; and then she suddenly asked me whether it was because of her and Gustave that I had remained faithful to their father. "For I have never doubted that you have remained faithful to him," she added, looking at me fixedly as one looks at a child one is reprimanding. However monstrous I thought this reversal of our roles, I protested that the idea of deceiving my husband had never entered my head for a moment; then she said she knew quite well that I had been in love with Bourgweilsdorf.

"If so, it was without my being aware of it," I retorted curtly.

But she went on: "You may not have owned it to yourself, but *he* was aware of it all right, I am certain."

I had risen, to get away from her, ready to leave the room if she went on talking in this way; in any case I was determined not to answer her any more. There was a short silence, and then I sat down again, or rather sank into another chair, for I felt at the end of my strength. She immediately flung herself once more into my arms, sat on my knee, and became more caressing than ever. "But, Mamma, do understand that I don't blame you."

And as these words made me start with indignation, she took hold of my two arms and held me a prisoner, laughing as though to lessen the intolerable impropriety of her words by making fun of them.

"I should just like to know," she went on, "whether there has been any sacrifice on your part."

She had once more become very serious; as for me, I did my best to keep an impassive countenance; she understood that I should not answer, and went on:

"What a good novel you might help me to write! It would be called 'The Duties of a Mother, or The Useless Sacrifice.'" And as I continued silent, she began to shake her head slowly. "No," she said, "it's not because you have made yourself the slave of your duty—" then she corrected herself: "of an imaginary duty. . . . No, no, you can see for yourself that I can't be grateful to you for that. No, don't protest. I really think I couldn't go on loving you if I felt under an obligation to you, if I felt that you thought I was under an obligation to you. Your virtue is your own; I do not choose to feel myself bound by it." Then suddenly changing her tone: "Now, quickly, say something, anything, so that when I go back to my room I may not be furious with myself for having spoken to you so."

I felt mortally sad and was only able to kiss her on the forehead.

I did not sleep last night. Geneviève's sentences re-echoed through the frightful emptiness of my heart. Ah! I ought not to have let her speak. For at present I do not know whether it was she who spoke or myself. Will that voice I have allowed to raise itself ever again be silent? If I am not more frightened, it is because my cowardice reassures me. My mind revolts in vain; in spite of myself I remain submissive. I ask myself in vain what else I could have done in life; in spite of myself I still remain attached to Robert, to my children, who are Robert's children. I look round for some way of escape, but I know well enough that if I had the liberty I long for, I should not know what to do with it. And the words Geneviève once said to me in fun sound like a knell in my ears:

"It's no good, my poor mamma; you'll never be anything but an honest woman."

22 July

I will write down my thoughts without order, as they come. . . .

My children's respect held me back and I liked to lean upon it. Geneviève has robbed me of this support. I have no longer even that to help me. At present it is with myself alone that I fight; it is of my own virtue that I am the irremediable prisoner.

If even I had any grievance against my husband! But no; those defects of his from which I suffer and which I have come to hate are not directed against me, and the only thing I can reproach him with is his very being. Not that any other love tempts me; I have no thought of betraying him—at any rate not otherwise than by going away. Oh! all I want is to leave him. . . .

If only he were an invalid! If only he could not do without me!

How can I renounce life before I am forty? Will not God grant me some duties other than this mortal effacement and wretched resignation?

What advice can I hope for? And from whom? My parents are lost in admiration of Robert and think I am perfectly happy. Why should I undeceive them? What can I hope for from them except perhaps pity, which I have no use for?

Abbé Bredel is too old to understand me. And what could he say to me more than he said at Arcachon, which merely increased my unhappiness—that I must do all in my power to hide their father's inferiority from the children? As if— But I will not speak to him of the conversation I have just had with Geneviève; it would only strengthen the opinion he has of her, which is not a good one; and I know that at the first words he uttered, I should take Geneviève's side. As for her, she never could bear the Abbé, and all I could ever obtain from her was that she should not be impertinent to him.

Marchant? . . . Yes, no doubt, *he* would understand me. He would understand me only too well. That is why I cannot speak to him. And then I could not forgive myself for disturbing Yvonne's happiness. I am too fond of her not to hide everything from her.

But as I write this, an idea has suddenly dawned upon me—an absurd idea perhaps, but none the less I feel it to be imperative: the person I must speak to about Robert is Robert himself. My mind is made up: I will speak to him this very evening.

23 July

Yesterday evening as I was preparing to go to Robert's room for the explanation that I had determined to have with him, Papa was announced. It is so unusual for him to come at such a late hour that my first impulse was to exclaim:

"Is anything the matter with Mamma?"

"Your mamma is perfectly well," he answered. And then as he pressed me in his arms, he went on: "You are the one who isn't well, my dear. No, no, no, don't deny it. I've been feeling for a long time past that something is amiss. . . . My poor little Éveline, I can't bear to feel that you are unhappy."

I began by saying:

"Everything is all right, Papa. What makes you think—?"

But I had to stop, for he put his two hands on my shoulders and looked at me so searchingly that I felt I was losing countenance.

"Those black rings round your eyes tell a very different story. Come, my darling—my dear little Éveline, what are you hiding from me? Is Robert deceiving you?"

This question was so unexpected that I exclaimed stupidly, as if in spite of myself:

"Oh! I wish to goodness he were!"

"What! It's something serious, then. Come, tell me: what's the matter?"

He was so pressing that I could restrain myself no longer.

"No, Robert is not deceiving me," I said. "I have nothing to reproach him with; and that's the very thing that is so dreadful." And as I saw that he did not understand: "Do you remember, when at first you opposed my marriage, I asked you then what you objected to in Robert, and I was indignant when you found nothing to answer? Why didn't you tell me?"

"Why, my little girl, I really don't know. It's such a long time ago. . . . Yes, I misjudged Robert at first. I disliked his ways. Happily, I soon understood that I was mistaken. . . ."

"Oh, Papa! Unfortunately you were right in your first judgment of him. You thought you were mistaken afterwards because I was happy with him. But it didn't last. It was my turn to understand. No, you were not mistaken. I ought to have listened to you at first, as I used to when I was a good little girl."

He stayed for a long time as if utterly overcome, shaking his head and murmuring: "You poor little thing! . . . You poor little thing!" so tenderly that I was miserable at causing him so much distress. But I had to go on to the end. Plucking up my courage, I said:

"I want to leave him."

He gave a violent start and exclaimed: "Heyday! Heyday!" in such an odd tone of voice that I should have laughed if I had had the heart to. Then he made me sit down close beside him on the sofa, stroking my hair as he spoke.

"Your Abbé would look rather queer if you did

such a silly thing as that. Have you talked to him about it?"

I nodded my head to signify I had and then was obliged to confess that I did not get on so well with the Abbé nowadays as I used to, which made him smile and give me a little mocking glance. The idea of this indirect victory over a person he could never abide seemed to amuse him very much.

"Dear! dear! dear!" Then changing his tone, he went on: "Let's talk seriously, my dear child—that is to say, practically."

Then he explained that if I left my husband's domicile, all the blame would attach to me.

"People as a rule only understand the value of a good reputation after they have lost it. My little Éveline was always one to have rather chimerical ideas. Where would you go? What would you do? No, no, you must go on living with Robert. Take him all in all, he is not a bad fellow. If you try to have an explanation with him, perhaps he might understand."

"He won't understand; but I'll speak to him all the same, and it'll only tighten the noose round my neck."

Then he went on to say that I must not try to escape, but "to establish a *modus vivendi*," to "find a working compromise." He likes using rather imposing words, as though to prove to himself that they don't frighten him. Then, no doubt with the intention of consoling me, he began to speak to me of my

mother and tell me that he had not found all he had
hoped for in marriage either. He had never confided
this to anyone, he told me, and he seemed extraordinarily relieved at being able at last to let himself
go—as he did to his heart's content. I had not the
courage to interrupt him, but his confidences made me
feel inexpressibly uncomfortable—as uncomfortable
as in my dreadful conversation with Geneviève. It
seems to me that it is not a good thing that commu-
nications of this kind should take place from one generation to another—that they do violence in one or
other of them to a feeling of intimate reserve which
it is no doubt better to respect.

My feeling of discomfort had yet another reason,
which I dislike mentioning, for I am too fond of Papa
not to be sorry to have to judge him and I wish I need
never find he was in the wrong—a reason about which
I should keep silent if I had not promised myself to be
sincere in these pages. When Papa began to talk to
me of his youthful ambitions and of everything he
thinks he might have done if he had felt himself
better understood and better seconded by my mother,
I could not refrain from thinking that it only rested
with him to have got more out of himself, and that if
he failed to make the most of his intelligence and his
gifts, it was not disagreeable to him to believe that
Mamma was responsible for this. I do not doubt that
he has suffered from Mamma's wholly practical and
narrow-minded point of view, but I think he is rather

pleased to be able to say: "Your mother doesn't wish . . . Your mother doesn't think . . ." and to rest content with that.

He told me afterward he did not know a single married couple whose union was so perfect that one of the parties had not sometimes wished never to have contracted it. I did not protest, for Papa does not like being contradicted, but I cannot accept such a statement, which seems to me a blasphemy.

Our conversation lasted till far on into the night. Papa was, I believe, greatly cheered by it and did not understand that he left me more deeply in despair than ever.

24 July

A running noose. . . . And every effort I make to free myself only serves to tighten it. . . . My final explanation with Robert has taken place. I have played my last card and lost. Ah! I should have gone away without saying a word to Papa or to anyone. I can do no more. I am beaten.

I found Robert lying on the sofa, for he began to leave his bed a few days ago.

"I came to see whether you wanted anything," I said, trying to think of some way of starting the conversation.

"No, thank you, dear," he answered in his most angelic voice. "I feel really better this evening and I am beginning to think that after all the angel of death has passed me by this time." Then, as he never misses an opportunity of showing his generosity, his sensibility, his greatness of soul: "I have given you a great deal of anxiety. I wish I was certain I deserve all the care that has been lavished on me."

I tried to look at him with indifference.

"Robert, I should like to have a serious conversation with you."

"You know very well, my dear, that I never refuse to speak seriously. When one has seen death at such close quarters as I have in the last few days, one is naturally inclined to have serious thoughts."

But I suddenly ceased to understand what I was complaining of and what I had come to say. Or, to be more accurate, what I was complaining of suddenly seemed to me impossible to formulate. And, above all, I could think of no sentence, no question, by which I could start; I was still, however, firmly resolved to engage in the struggle and repeated to myself until my brain seemed in a whirl: "If you don't do it now, you'll never do it." Then I thought that it probably did not much matter with what sentence I began the attack, and that the best thing would be to trust to a kind of inspiration, which could not fail eventually to come to my help.

So, like a diver who plunges, eyes shut, into the abyss, "Robert," I said, "I should like you to tell me, if you still remember, what reasons you had for marrying me."

Certainly he expected a question of this kind so little that for a moment he looked completely taken aback. For a moment only, for, whatever may be the situation in which circumstances place him, Robert is always extraordinarily prompt and clever at recovering himself. He reminds me of those little toy tumblers with pith heads which, however one throws them down, always settle again on their feet.

While he was looking at me to try to understand what purpose was hidden in my words, so as to adapt his defense to meet them, "What makes you speak of reason," he asked, "about a matter of feeling?"

Robert always manages to get the upper hand of his adversary. Whatever one does, the point of view in which he places himself immediately seems the superior one. I felt, as at a game of chess, that I was going to lose the advantage of the attack. It would be better to put him again on the defensive.

"Please try to speak to me simply."

He protested immediately: "It is impossible to speak more simply than I am doing."

It was true and I at once felt the imprudence of my words. They were full of an old grudge that had, no doubt, had time to grow big in my heart; but this once there was no ground for it.

"Yes, you say that simply. But as a rule your loftiness is overwhelming; you like to take refuge in regions so sublime that you know I shall never be able to follow you there."

"It seems to me, my dear," he said, smiling affably and in his suavest tone of voice, "that for the moment it is you who are not being simple. Look, tell me straight out: you have something to reproach me with. I am listening."

But now it was I who was assuming Robert's manner, Robert's way of expressing himself, which had become so unbearable to me—just as, when I was younger, I used to put on an English accent out of sympathy when I was talking with an Englishman, to Papa's great amusement. Was it for the same reason that Robert, when he spoke to me, found himself as though forced to speak simply, while I, in talking to him, irresistibly adopted his tone and his style? I plunged deeper and deeper into the bog.

"If I could only reproach you with anything definite, what a relief it would be!" I managed to say. "But no! I know only too well that you never put yourself in the wrong, as I did just now when I began to explain myself. And yet I assure you I am not giving way to a thoughtless impulse. This conversation that I have been meaning to have for such a long time past and that I have been putting off from day to day—" I could not finish my sentence—it was too long already. I went on in so low a voice that I was surprised he could hear me:

"Listen, Robert. It's simply that I can't go on living with you any longer."

In order to find strength to say this, even in a

whisper, I had been obliged to stop looking at him. But as he was silent, I raised my eyes. I thought he had turned pale.

"If I were to ask you in my turn what reasons you have for leaving me," he finally said, "you might answer, like me, that it's a matter, not of reason, but of feeling."

"You see that I don't say so," I answered.

But he: "Éveline, am I to understand that you don't love me any more?"

His voice trembled just enough to leave me in doubt whether his emotion was sincere or feigned. I made a great effort and said painfully:

"The man I passionately loved was very different from the man I have slowly discovered you to be."

He raised his eyebrows and shoulders. "If you speak in riddles, I can't—"

I went on: "I have gradually discovered that you are very different from what I thought you were at first—from the man I once loved."

Then something extraordinary happened: I saw him suddenly put his head in his hands and burst into sobs. There could be no question of feigning; they were real sobs, which shook his whole body; real tears, which wet his fingers and ran down his cheeks, while he repeated wildly a dozen times over:

"My wife doesn't love me! My wife doesn't love me! . . ."

I was far from expecting this explosion. It struck

me dumb—not that I was much moved myself, for it
is obvious that I no longer love Robert. I was indignant, on the contrary, at seeing him have recourse to
weapons that I thought disloyal; I was uncomfortable
too at feeling that I was the cause of a real grief, before which my grievances must needs give way. In
order to console Robert I should have had to make
use of lying protestations. I drew near him and put
my hand on his forehead, which he raised at once.

"But why should I have married you, then? Was
it for your name? Your fortune? Your parents' situation? Was it? Was it? Say something so that I may
understand. You know well that—that I—"

He seemed at present so natural, so perfectly sincere, that I expected to hear him say: "that I might
have found a much better match." But the words that
came were: "that it was because I loved you"; then,
in a voice once more broken with sobs: ". . . and because I thought—that—you loved me."

I was almost shocked by my own indifference. However sincere Robert's emotion now was, the exhibition of that emotion froze me.

"I thought I should be the only one to suffer from
this explanation," I began; but he interrupted me.

"You say I am not the man you thought. But, then,
you are not the woman I thought, either. How is it
possible ever to know if one really is the person one
thinks one is?"

It is a habit of his to seize hold of other people's

ideas and twist them round so as to serve his own purposes (I really think he does it quite unconsciously) ; so he went on:

"But not one of us, my poor dear, not one of us can constantly keep on the heights where he would wish to be. The whole drama of our moral life is that —exactly that. I don't know whether you follow me." (He has an invariable trick of saying these words whenever he begins to change his subject and realizes that his interlocutor is aware of it.) "It is only people without an ideal who—"

"Robert, Robert," I said gently, with a restraining movement of my hand, for I knew that, once started on such an elevated theme, he would never stop of his own accord. My interruption made him slightly shift his ground.

"As if one was not always forced to climb down a little in life! . . . I mean one is always forced to bring one's ideal down to somewhere within one's reach. But as for you, your ideals have always been chimerical."

(So, then, it must be true, since Papa said the same thing yesterday.) Then, with a natural rebound, Robert soared up again into the lofty regions from which my egotistical sigh had impertinently snatched him.

"And there, my dear, you touch upon a problem of the highest interest—the problem of expression itself. The question is, you see, whether emotion exhausts itself in the expression of emotion, or whether, on the contrary, it is called into being by the expression, comes, as it were, to *inform* the expression. And indeed one almost begins to doubt whether anything exists in reality apart from its appearance, and whether— Let me just explain; you'll understand in a minute."

This last sentence always comes to the rescue when he begins to get confused. It irritates me more than anything.

"I understand perfectly well," I interrupted. "You mean it would be mad of me to mind whether you really feel all the fine feelings you express."

His glance grew suddenly charged with a kind of hatred.

"Oh!" he exclaimed in a voice that was almost strident, "it's a pleasure indeed to be understood by you. So that is the only impression our conversation has left on you? I let myself go; I speak to you with more confidence and frankness than I have ever done to anyone; I humble myself before you; I burst into tears before you. But my tears don't touch you the least in the world; you put your own interpretation on my words, and in an icy tone you give me to understand that all the feeling is on your side, and that all my love for you is nothing but—"

He was again interrupted for a moment by his sobs. I rose with only one thought in my head—to put an end to an interview that I had conducted so badly, which was ending in my discomfiture and in which I had only succeeded in putting myself to all appearance entirely in the wrong. As I laid my hand on his arm to say good-by, he turned round abruptly and the words burst from him:

"No, I say, no, no. It isn't true. You are wrong. If you still loved me in the least, you would understand that I am only a poor creature struggling like all of us and trying as best he can to become a little better than he is."

He had suddenly found the words most capable of touching me. I bent over him to kiss him, but he pushed me away almost brutally.

"No, no. Let me alone. I can only see, only feel, one thing—that you have ceased to love me."

On these words I left him, my heart weighed down with a fresh unhappiness—an unhappiness that confronts his own, which his own has revealed to me. Alas, he loves me still! I cannot leave him.

EPILOGUE

I HAD resolved to write nothing more in this book. Very shortly after the conversation with Robert that I have related, our personal preoccupations were swept away by the terrible events that have overwhelmed Europe. I wish I could recover the convictions of my childhood so that I might pray God with all my heart: O God! protect France! But I imagine the Christians of Germany pray the same God in the same way for their country, in spite of everything we hear about them that might make us think them barbarians. It is in the virtue of each of us, of all of us such as we are, that France must find her protection, her defense. I thought at first that Robert was profoundly convinced of this. I witnessed his grief at being unable to serve on account of his convalescence; then, a few months later, I know that he consulted Marchant as to how he could get a medical certificate to permit him to enlist. Unfortunately, I learned soon after that his class was about to be called up, that he ran the risk of being transferred from the auxiliary to the active army, and that by enlisting beforehand he would be free to choose the branch of the service he preferred—which he did with the utmost precaution and with the help of all the influence he could command. Why repeat all this here? I wish only to relate the dreadful scene I have just had with him, which has made me make my final decision. But how can I explain this without referring first to the fresh medical board which he had to go up to, where he managed to get himself discharged as suffering from "chronic cephalalgia resulting from traumatism"? It was then that I wanted to leave for one of the hospitals at the front, where I was certain of having my services accepted; but Robert's authorization was necessary. He refused them to me brutally, with many hard words, saying that I only wanted to go in order to mortify him, to set him an example, to shame him. . . . I was obliged to give in, to wait, and finally to content myself with the Lariboisière Hospital in Paris, where I often spent the night, so that I saw him only very rarely. I was astounded one morning to find him again in miltary uniform. Thanks to his knowledge of English, he had succeeded in being taken on by an American war-relief committee, and this enabled him to wear a uniform without being actually in the army, and to assume a martial air. But poor Robert had no luck; his patriotic speeches soon led to his being selected for service at Verdun. As it was impossible to get out of this decently, he "thought it his duty" to put a good face on it, so much so that he was shortly given the *Croix de guerre*, to the great admiration of Gustave, my parents, and quantities of friends, who went into ecstasies. At Verdun itself, where he sent for me to go and see him, he managed to pass as a hero. I think he was merely waiting for this decoration to get sent home, which, thanks to the influence he possesses, he was able to do without much difficulty. As I expressed surprise at this sudden return, which agreed very ill with the fine speeches about constancy and fortitude I heard him make a short time before at Verdun itself, he explained that he knew from an unimpeachable source that the war was on the point of coming to an end, and that he felt he could at present be more useful in Paris, where the morale appeared to him less good than at the front.

This was two days ago. . . . And yet I have uttered no reproaches. Since our painful explanation I accept everything from him without saying a word. It is not so much his actions that I despise as the reasons he gives for them. Perhaps he read my contempt in my eyes. He suddenly became resentful. His decoration no longer allows him to doubt the authenticity of his virtues and at the same time permits him to dispense with them. I, who have no *Croix de guerre*, have need of virtue itself, for its own sake, and not for the approbation it brings us. "Chimerical" creature that I am, I have need of reality. . . .

After having naïvely congratulated himself on having come through the war at so small a cost, and seeing that I could not repress a smile, "As if you wouldn't have done exactly the same thing yourself!" he suddenly exclaimed.

No, Robert, I cannot allow you to say this; I cannot, above all, allow you to think it. I did not answer, but my mind was instantly made up. I managed to see Marchant that same evening and settle everything with him. He was good enough to take the necessary steps for me. Tomorrow I shall go off quietly to Châtellerault. In the hospital there behind the lines I shall have the appearance of being in perfect safety. That is what I want. Geneviève alone knows the truth. How did she find out the kind of illness that is nursed there? I do not know. . . . She implored me to let her come too and take service at my side. But I cannot endure that she should expose herself to such risks at her age; she has all her life before her. "No, Geneviève, you cannot, you must not follow where I am going," I said, kissing her very tenderly, as though to say good-by. My dear Geneviève is not satisfied with appearances either. I love her dearly. I am writing this for her to read. It is to her that I bequeath this book if I should not return.

ROBERT

TO

ERNEST ROBERT CURTIUS

Cuverville
5 September 1929

MY DEAR FRIEND:

In a letter you wrote me after reading my School for Wives, *you expressed your regret at knowing my "heroine's" husband only through his wife's journal.*

"How much one would like," you wrote, "to have some observations of Robert's as a companion piece to Éveline's diary."

This little book responds perhaps to your appeal. It is but natural that it should be dedicated to you.

PART

i

SIR:

Although my first feeling on reading your *School for Wives* was one of indignation, I will not permit myself to bear you a personal grudge. You have thought fit to hand over to the public a woman's private diary—a diary she would never have contemplated writing could she for one moment have suspected the use it would one day be put to. Confessions, indiscreet revelations, are the fashion of the day; they are published regardless of the material and moral damage their indiscretion may cause the survivors; regardless too of their deplorable example. I leave it to your conscience (for we all have one) to consider whether it was really your duty to aid and abet a publication so particularly offensive to a third party and, under cover of your name, to derive from it glory—and profit. My daughter, you will answer, invited you to do so. I will say later on what I think of her conduct. I know from other sources, as well as from your own confessions, that you are inclined to attach more weight to the opinions of young people than to those of their parents. You are of course free to do so; but on this occasion we see where such a course leads, and where it would lead if more people were like you—which God forbid! Enough.

Will you be greatly astonished if I tell you that I am not the only person who fails to recognize my likeness to the inconsequent, vain, shallow individual portrayed by my wife. "To resent an insult," says some ancient author, "is to admit that it has struck home." But even if the insult had struck home, I should be the only one to know it, as my name has never been mentioned in this connection. If I say all this, it is to make your readers understand that it is in no way from a desire to rehabilitate myself that I now take up my pen, but purely from a regard for truth, for justice, and for accuracy.

An opinion is more easily arrived at, but also more unfairly, after hearing a single witness than when one lends an ear to contrary evidence. Since you have given *The School for Wives* the protection of your name, I here offer you *The School for Husbands;* and I call upon you, in the name of your professional dignity, to publish the following refutation in the same conditions of letterpress and publicity as that volume.

But before embarking on my subject, I appeal to all honorable people. What do they think, I ask, of a young girl who immediately after her mother's death takes possession of that mother's private papers, without giving her father any opportunity of looking through them? You have somewhere written, I remember: "I have a horror of honest folk," and no doubt you sanction and applaud such daring actions as enable you to recognize the influence of your own teaching. In my daughter's shameless audacity I see the melancholy result of the "liberal" education my wife thought fit to give our two children. My great error was to have given way to her, as was my habit, from a dislike of being autocratic and a horror of arguments. Those that arose between us upon this subject were of extreme gravity, and I am surprised to find no mention of them in her diary. I will return to this later on.

Let no one expect me, however, to take up every one of the points upon which my wife's testimony seems to me to be erroneous. And in particular certain insinuations that I should consider it beneath my dignity to answer—those that refer to my courage, patriotism, and conduct during the war. For that matter, Éveline does not seem to realize that her doubt whether I really deserved my *Croix de guerre* necessarily casts an aspersion upon either the integrity or the competence of the chiefs who bestowed it. Did I really say the words she puts in my mouth? I sincerely believe not. Or if I did, they were not spoken in the tone or with the intention that she so maliciously gives them. In any case, I have no recollection of them. Nor on my side do I accuse her of having deliberately and consciously falsified my character. (I accuse her of nothing.) But I believe that a certain degree of what the English so aptly call "prejudice" makes us actually hear other people say what we expect them to say, so that we get from them, to some extent, words that it is not even necessary for our memory to misrepresent.

What, on the other hand, I remember very well is that I felt that Éveline had reached a point when, whatever might be the words I used, they would always convey the same impression to her. She could not hear me tell anything but lies.

But it is not, as I have said, my intention to defend myself. I prefer to relate in my turn and in all simplicity my recollections of our life in common. I shall speak in particular of those twenty years which her diary passes over in silence. My task is an arduous one, for as I write I seem to feel the reader leaning over my shoulder on the look-out for the least word that will reveal my "deceitfulness," my "duplicity," etc. (these are the expressions the critics used). And yet if I am too careful of my writing, I run the risk of distorting the lines of my character and of falling into the snare of affectation at the very moment and for the very reason that I am endeavoring to avoid it. . . . The difficulty is no mean one. I shall only, I think, overcome it by not thinking of it, by writing straight on, *currente calamo*, and by starting afresh, without taking into account anything Éveline may have written or the public thought about me. May I not then have some small right to hope that the public will do the same thing by me—that is, not bring to the reading of these lines a mind too exclusively made up beforehand?

There is another thing that disturbs me, I must confess. The critics have vied with one another in praising my wife's style. I was indeed far from suspecting that Éveline wrote so well. I had no means of judging, for, as we always lived together, she had no occasion to write letters to me. People have even gone so far as to suppose—superlative praise indeed!—that the diary was written by you, M. Gide, who . . .* Certainly the pages that follow can aspire to no such distinction. If in my youth I nursed perhaps some literary pretensions, I soon relinquished them (to speak like you). And, apropos, can you tell me why all the critics (such of them as I have read, at any rate) represent me as a second-rate poet, when not only have I never written a line of verse (at least, since I was a boy at school, when I hammered out a few laborious sonnets), but moreover never had the slightest desire to write one? Is it my fault if Éveline at first thought me more gifted than I actually was? And can one have a legitimate grievance against a person for not being Racine or Pindar simply because a lovesick girl took him for such? . . . I should like to expatiate upon this point, because I believe that this is the reason for cruel disappointments, in friendship as well as in love: not to see the other person at once as he really is, but to begin by making

* Three lines omitted.

a kind of idol of him, and then to be angry with him
for not coming up to the mark, as if the poor wretch
could help it. For that matter, I did not at first see
Éveline as she was either. But what was she? She
did not know herself. She was the woman I loved.
And as long as she loved me, she tried to resemble my
idol and adorned herself with the virtues I believed
her to possess and which she knew would please me.
As long as she loved me she was not concerned to
know herself; her one desire was to lose herself in
me. . . . But we touch here, I believe, upon a problem of very general and very serious interest. I shall
write what follows in an attempt to elucidate it. I
first wish, however, to give a short account of myself
as I was before I knew her. This will, I think, help
people to understand what Éveline stood for in my
eyes.

My childhood was not a happy one. My father
kept an ironmonger's shop in one of the busiest streets
of Perpignan. I was only twelve when he died, leaving the burden of carrying on the business to my
mother, who was not a very good business woman,
and who had, I think, a dishonest head clerk. My
sister, who was two years younger than I, had delicate
health and we lost her a few years later. I was brought
up between these two women, associating very little
with boys of my own age, whom I thought for the
most part stupid and vulgar, and having hardly any

other amusement than a weekly visit to an old unmarried aunt, who lived in a kind of large farmhouse
two miles out of Perpignan, and with whom we used
to lunch every Sunday. My sister and I petted her
dogs and cats and fished for goldfish in a small oblong
pond at the end of her little garden, while my mother
and my aunt watched us from a distance. We used
to bait our lines with breadcrumbs, because we
thought worms repulsive and were afraid of dirtying
ourselves—for which reason we always came away
discomfited. This, however, did not prevent us from
beginning again the following Sunday, and we never
left our rods until our aunt called us in to tea. After
tea a game of lotto kept us occupied till it was time to
leave. The old barouche that had been sent to fetch
us in the morning took us back to Perpignan in time
for dinner.

This aunt, who died the same year as my sister,
left us her fortune, which turned out unexpectedly
large; this enabled my mother to retire after having
disposed of the business, and permitted me to continue my studies.

I was a fairly good pupil. Why should I hesitate
to say very good? It is because application is not
nowadays the fashion; genius is more in favor. My
application was extraordinary and I cannot remember a time when I was not wholly dominated by a
sense of duty. And besides I loved my mother and
wanted to spare her every anxiety I could. Before my

aunt's legacy my education would have been impossible but for a scholarship I managed to carry off.
Our life was inexpressibly monotonous and dreary,
and it would be no pleasure for me to recall the past
if it were not for the gentle figures of my mother and
my sister, who bounded the whole of my heart's horizon. They were both very pious. My religion formed
part, I think, of my love for them. I went with them
to Mass every Sunday, before the barouche came to
take us to my aunt's. I listened with great docility to
the exhortations and advice of Father X, who took
an interest in all three of us, and I was careful not to
indulge in any thoughts that I should not have been
able to tell him or that he would not have been able
to approve.

My sister was sixteen when she died; I was eighteen
at the time. I had just finished my first schooling and
my aunt's legacy might have enabled me to take some
courses in Paris; but the thought of my mother's
loneliness if I went so far made me prefer Toulouse,
which was near enough to permit of my frequently
returning to Perpignan. Though preparing my first
law examinations, I still had a considerable amount
of leisure and my one thought was to spend as much
of it as I could with my mother. I read a good deal,
but it was as easy to read at home. After my aunt's
death my mother saw no one but me. My sister's
image always made an invisible third between us; it
accompanied me everywhere, and I think it is to that

as much as to Father X's counsels that I owe my horror of the facile pleasures into which my companions were so easily led. Toulouse is a large enough town to offer dissipated young men many opportunities of falling into sin. And at this moment I protest, as I have never failed to protest, against the modern theory that tends to underrate our virtue by maintaining that the only desires that can be resisted are those that are not in reality particularly strong. I am willing to believe, however, that the assistance of religion is indispensable to human weakness. I sought it. And for this reason I take no pride in my resistance. Moreover, I avoided dangerous amusements, bad companions, and licentious reading. I should not, indeed, have mentioned this subject if it had not been necessary to give some idea of what Mlle X became to me as soon as I met her. I was waiting for her.

I realize, indeed, at the present time how dangerous such a form of waiting may prove. A young man, as pure as by God's help I then was, who suddenly concentrates all his latent aspirations on one only woman is in danger of idealizing that woman to excess. But is not that the distinguishing feature of love? Moreover, Éveline was worthy of the worship I laid at her feet, and I congratulated myself on not having squandered the riches of my heart, which I was able to offer her intact.

After having passed my examinations with some

distinction, I left Toulouse, where I no longer found sufficient food for my intellectual curiosities. I have said that the idea of duty had governed my life since my earliest childhood. But I was obliged to consider that if I had duties toward my mother, I had equally sacred ones toward my country—which is equivalent to saying toward myself, whose sole thought was to serve it well. Set free from all anxiety about money matters, I was at liberty to dispose of my time in my own way. Painting and literature attracted me, but I did not think I possessed gifts striking enough, or at any rate exclusive enough, to take up the career of either an artist or a novelist. It seemed to me that my proper role in this world would be rather to assist other people in making the most of themselves and to contribute to the triumph of such ideas as I might be convinced were of real value. Let those who will, despise this modest ambition. As soon as I had finished my term of military service, which I spent in the artillery, I set about finding out my own special line of usefulness. What was it that France stood most in need of? This was the question I made it my business to examine and I began to frequent the people in Paris who I thought would be best able to instruct me and those who felt the same indignation as myself at the state of blindness, carelessness, and disorder in which our country was losing her health and strength.

My father-in-law was astonished later on that I

had not "launched out," as he said, into politics, in
which, he declared, I should certainly have made my
way. His regrets on this subject were all the more
meritorious as I by no means shared his opinions. He
considered the present state of things, not indeed as
perfect, but as perfectly acceptable, and, like Philinte
in *The Misanthrope,* resigned himself to what he
called the inevitable. As for me, I considered, and still
consider, that the first step toward improvement is to
hold the opinion that our political situation, on which
everything else depends, must of necessity undergo
a change. And was it not natural enough to apply to
my country the precepts that guided my own behavior and had been of so much benefit to me?

Politics, in my opinion, were too much a matter of
expediency. They would have obliged me to accept
compromises and to swerve from my established line
of conduct. But this is not a justification of myself
that I am writing—it is my story.

I frequented a great number of writers and artists.
My firmness of character was exercised in resisting
the temptation to follow in their wake and become
a writer or a painter myself, as would have been my
natural bent. In this way I retained greater scope for
appreciating and helping forward other people's
work, not only by advice (which is often least welcomed by those who need it most), but by a certain
amount of support, which my acquaintances in the
political world enabled me to command (not to men-

tion the more direct assistance I often used to give when I was sure the artist would not be encouraged by it to a life of idleness).

All those who have made our country the object of their serious study have come to the conclusion that its original elements are good and that what is chiefly missing is the capacity for turning them to account—a quality in which our German neighbors excel. Man requires to be directed, supported, ruled. What should I myself have been worth if I had not accepted the guidance of two or three ruling ideas and principles that far too many people nowadays attempt to shake off like a troublesome yoke.

In order to explain the kind of activities I entered upon, the best plan will be to give an example; I will choose one that gave some of the most striking and highly appreciated results.

It had often occurred to me that the best books, in consequence of their authors' lack of skill and enterprise in practical matters, have great difficulty in reaching the select public they merit. That, on the contrary, a great number of well-intentioned but insufficiently informed readers pass by food for the mind that is really wholesome, in order to browse upon works having often very little to recommend them, merely because they have been brought into view at an opportune moment by skillful advertisement. I thought I could be of real service both to the public I mention, to the authors, and to their pub-

lishers. I pointed out to these last the advantages of
a scheme of mine which at once interested them. I
constituted a jury, selected from among the highest-
minded men of the day, whose business it was to
designate periodically the books that merited the consideration of persons able to realize that the recom-
mendations of such a jury afforded an unparalleled
guarantee. Frenchmen are so much the creatures of
habit, so confident of their own taste, so accessible
to the lure of fashion, that I found it very difficult
to persuade them to trust the judgment of competent
authorities. Nevertheless, by bestirring myself, I
managed to recruit a sufficient number of subscribers
to ensure the success of certain works, as well as of
the scheme itself. By this means I protected my élite
of readers from second-rate or debasing books, which,
needless to say, my jury refrained from mentioning;
for it is to be remarked that a mind filled with good
literature has not much appetite left for bad. The
services I thus rendered were not, alas, appreciated
by my wife. At every fresh meeting of the jury Éveline ironically inquired, not after the titles of the
chosen books, but after the menu of the lunch that
preceded the deliberations—an excellent lunch, it is
true, which was offered by the publishers and to which
the members of the jury were always kind enough to
invite me.

As for the books selected, Éveline affected to have
no wish to read them or else to know them already;

it was by the independence of her judgment that I was best able to gauge the decline of her love. But here we enter into the heart of the matter.

This is not a diary I am writing. The events I group together were spread over a great number of years. I cannot tell exactly how long ago it was that Éveline first began to show signs of this unsubmissive temper, which, notwithstanding all my love for her, I was obliged to blame. Unsubmissiveness is always blameworthy, but I hold it particularly so in a woman. During the first years of our marriage, and still more at the time of our engagement, Éveline espoused my opinions and ideas without inquiry and with so much warmth and such perfect ease that no one could have imagined that those opinions and ideas were not naturally her own. As for her tastes in literature and painting, one would have said that they had been waiting for me to form them, for her parents understood very little of such matters. We were therefore in perfect agreement. It was not till much later that I understood how it was that this agreement of ours came to be disturbed—not till too late, indeed, when the irreparable mischief had been done.

In spite of their advanced views, which they did not hesitate to express in public, I still continued to offer the hospitality of our hearth and home to two of our friends—Dr. Marchant and the painter Burgweilsdorf—the latter on account of his great talent, which at that time I was almost alone to recognize, and the former because of his scientific attainments, and also because he had on occasion been of some service to us. I do not believe in spontaneous generation, and especially not in the minds of women; you may be quite certain that the ideas they develop have been sown in them by others. I am here ready to acknowledge my error; I ought not to have received in my house such avowed freethinkers, nor have allowed them, in spite of all their learning and all their talent, to speak of their opinions—at any rate in Éveline's presence. She does not conceal in her diary the interest with which she regarded them, and as they were my friends, I was at first foolish enough to be glad of it. It is beneath my character to be jealous, and to tell the truth, Éveline, thank Heaven, gave me no reason to be so; but it was more than enough that she should listen with such approbation to their talk. On the other hand, she stopped listening to Father Bredel, whose words would at least have made a happy counterweight to theirs. Then discussions arose between us. As she read a great deal and, disdaining my advice, chose books of a kind to encourage her to boldness, she no longer scrupled to hold her own against me.

Our discussions bore particularly upon the subject of the children's education.

I have had many occasions to observe the havoc caused by freethinking in married life and the disputes it foments between husband and wife. Gen-

erally it is the husband who abjures the faith of his
fathers and gives way in consequence to unbridled
licentiousness. But I believed, at any rate as far as
the children are concerned, the evil is still greater
when it is the woman who emancipates herself, for
the woman's role is eminently a conservative one. I
tried in vain to make Éveline understand this, beg-
ging her to consider the responsibility she was thus
assuming—as regards her daughter in particular, for
the joy was granted me of seeing my son prefer his
father's counsels. As for Geneviève, who was more
eager for instruction than Gustave, and more curious
than beseems a woman, her mind was only too naturally inclined to follow her mother's down the slip-
pery path of unbelief. Under pretense of preparing
her for her examinations, Éveline encouraged her in
a course of reading that deeply grieved Father Bredel
and made me protest against the education that is
nowadays given to women, which is for the most part
of very poor service to them. I think their brains are
not formed for this kind of nourishment and do not
furnish the natural antidote to the poisons it breeds.
I protested in vain and ended by giving way, weary
of fighting and desirous of preserving the peace of our
married life, which was already seriously threatened.
The results of this education have, alas, justified all
my forebodings. But as Geneviève's most disastrous
lapses of conduct took place after my wife's death,
this is not the place in which to speak of them, and

the subject is one on which it would be particularly painful for me to dwell.

Yes, as I have said and as I repeat, I consider that the woman's role in the home and in civilization at large is and should be conservative. And it is only when the woman fully realizes this that the man's mind can feel sufficiently disengaged to push forward on its own account. How often have I felt that the position taken up by Éveline hampered the real progress of my own mind by forcing me to assume a function in our married life that should by rights have been hers. On the other hand, I am grateful to her before God for having thus encouraged me in the practice of my duties, religious as well as social, and fortified me in my faith. And this is why before God I pardon her.

I touch here on a point that is particularly delicate, but I believe it to be of such importance that I shall be perhaps forgiven for dwelling on it with some insistence. That freshness, that virginity of soul as well as of body which every man worthy of the name hopes to find in the young girl he chooses to be his mate were offered me in the most exquisite manner by Éveline. Could I have suspected—did she herself know—her true nature, and that when it ceased to be governed by love it would turn out to have so much in it that was refractory and self-willed? The specific quality of human love is to blind us to our own faults as well as to those of the loved one; I thought at first (we no doubt both thought) that the submission I so much admired in Éveline was a natural quality, when in reality it was due merely to love. For that matter, I did not require any other kind of submission from her than that which I demanded from my own mind. But that "obedience of the spirit" which, as Monseigneur de La Serre quite recently declared, is "perhaps more difficult to obtain than a reform of life," adding with great truth: "One is not a Christian without it" *—this submission of the intellect, which should be that of every good Catholic, was a thing Éveline soon ceased to have any pretensions to. Her pretension, on the contrary, was that she had enough personal judgment to be able to guide herself and to do without a director—and this just at the time when her recalcitrant spirit, which had hitherto lain dormant, began to awake and to subject the guiding principles of my life to a critical examination—that is to say, to cast doubt on them. She explained to me one day that our idea of Truth was no doubt not the same, and that while I continued to believe in a divine truth, exterior to mankind, revealed and transmitted under the eye and by the inspiration of God, she could no longer bring herself to consider anything true that she did not recognize as such herself; and this in spite of my telling her that this belief in a personal truth led straight to individualism and opened the door to anarchy.

* *Études,* 20 July 1929.

"My poor dear, how like you to have married an anarchist!" she answered, smiling. As if there were anything to smile at!

And it was not as though she kept her opinions to herself. No, she must needs sow their germs in the minds of our children—of my daughter in particular, who absorbed them only too readily and seemed to think that the sole end of education was to encourage freethinking.

Such demoralizing ideas, which in an inexperienced and unguarded mind, such as my wife's mind was, make their way slowly and surely, are comparable to the termites of tropical countries, which undermine and disintegrate whole structures with astonishing rapidity. To all appearance the rafters remain the same and there is still no outward sign of decay, when the inside is already completely eaten away. Then, without a moment's warning, the edifice crumbles into dust.

Fragile indeed was the resting-place of my love! If I could have realized it in time, I might have taken measures to stamp out the evil, insisted on greater submission, forbidden certain books of whose insidious and dangerous influence I should have been more aware if I had begun by reading them myself. But I have always thought that the best way of avoiding evil is to turn aside one's eyes from it. This was not the case, I am sorry to say, with Éveline, who considered herself able to form her own opinions all by

herself. I here reproach myself keenly for a certain
weakness in my character; but precisely perhaps because I had a respect for authority—especially for the
Church's—and because I had the habit of submission,
I could not bring myself to exercise an act of marital
authority, though (as Father Bredel advised) it is
the duty of a husband who is steadfast in his faith to
assume such authority, and though it would no doubt
have stayed Éveline in her downward course. But I
did not understand how necessary this exercise of
authority was until the opportune moment for it had
gone by, and it might have been met with a sacri-
legious resistance. My eyes were opened one evening
when I was reading aloud to her; for at that time I
had not given up all hope of at any rate counter-
balancing the evil effect of those books I did not
venture—such was my weakness—to forbid her. I
was reading her the fine biographical notice of Count
Joseph de Maistre written by his son, which is to be
found in a volume of the Count's posthumous works.
Éveline, who had not been very well and had been
obliged to spend a few days in bed, was beginning to
get up again, but was still lying on the sofa. The same
lamp lighted my book and a small garment she was
embroidering in readiness for the birth of our second
child. It was in 1899. Geneviève was then two years
old. Her entrance into the world had been easy. But
the prospects in Gustave's case were less favorable.
Éveline's fatigue seemed abnormal; there was a very

unpleasant appearance of puffiness in her features, caused no doubt by a little albumen.

"How can you still love anyone so ugly?" she asked; and I at once protested that I saw her soul in her eyes and that *that* could not change. But I was obliged to admit to myself that the expression of her eyes was not what it had been and that her soul had become a stranger to me. I still sought to find love in it; but what I felt most was a spirit of resistance and sometimes almost of opposition. This opposition, which I still refused to admit to myself, suddenly manifested itself that evening in a particularly un-pleasant manner. At a moving passage of my reading Éveline suddenly let go her embroidery, seized her handkerchief, and put it to her lips so as almost to hide her face in it. She was laughing! I put down my book and looked at her steadily.

"Forgive me," she said. "I tried to stop myself, but it was stronger than I." And her shoulders were shaken by a fit of silly laughter it was only too ob-vious she could not control.

"I don't see what anyone can find comic in—" I began, at my calmest, and even with a shade of aston-ishment and severity.

She did not allow me to finish.

"Oh, there's nothing comic in what you are read-ing," she said; "quite the contrary. But it's your tone of profound conviction. . . ."

I must here quote the sentence that caused this unseemly and unbridled merriment on my wife's part:

"The whole time that young Joseph de Maistre passed at Turin attending law lectures at the university, he never allowed himself to read a single book without first writing home to Chambéry to ask his father's or mother's permission."

"I feel," she went on, "that you are simply longing to make me feel that that's admirable."

"And I see that I am very far from succeeding," I said with more sadness than annoyance. "Then *you* think it's ridiculous?"

"Supremely!"

She had stopped laughing and in her turn looked at me gravely, almost sadly; and it was I who turned aside my eyes for fear of discovering in that look of hers sentiments of which I could not approve. I wanted, however, to be conciliatory, as I know women must always be treated with gentleness, and that to ask too much is to risk losing all.

"Count de Maistre is an example," I said, "of what might be called an extremity case. That indeed is what makes his importance and his greatness. I admire his unyielding, uncompromising nature. What a striking contrast to the rest of mankind, who are always ready to make every kind of concession! There are too many men who resign themselves to the present laxness of morals, who make the best of it—which is another way of contributing to it. But I admit that we cannot demand of others the virtues to which we ourselves aspire."

"At any rate, it is exceedingly well put," she conceded, laughing again, but this time with a frank and cordial laughter, the like of which I was very seldom to hear again; for it soon lost that pure and charming quality and grew charged with irony—with something I refused at first to acknowledge as contempt—with something I long called merely a feeling of superiority, though even that is always a little shocking in a woman. However that may be, the cordiality of her laugh now reassured me. I wanted to show myself conciliatory.

"You have lately," I said, "allowed yourself great freedom in your reading; I trust you will not allow our children the same."

"I trust," she answered sharply, "our children will take it for themselves."

There was defiance in her voice and I felt these words went beyond her real meaning. I was determined to consider them as no more than idle pleasantry, but at the same time I felt it my duty to answer her.

"Fortunately I am here," I said with some severity. "It is the parents' task to protect their children. They might taste of poison unawares; they might give way to morbid curiosity."

She interrupted me:

"*You* have always made want of curiosity a virtue."

"I see its dangers sufficiently in you," I went on. "Men should feel curiosity for what will strengthen them in their faith, not for what may shatter it."

Éveline did not formulate the protest that obviously rose to her lips. I saw them shut and tighten as if to keep down a pressure from inside, as if to thrust back into herself thoughts that for the future she meant to hide and withdraw from the possibility of my attacks. I too said nothing, for, in the face of her silence, what more could I do but pray to God and the Holy Virgin that they would undertake the task I felt slipping from my grasp? And this I did that very evening with a full heart.

Our conversation was longer than I have recorded, for I remember having also said on the same evening in connection with Joseph de Maistre and his submission to his parents' judgment: "Men must always obey someone or something. It is better to obey God than one's own passions or instincts." This remark had been suggested to me by some reflections of Father Bredel's, and as they are not my own, I may perhaps be allowed to quote them as a perfect example of the profundity to which a respectful and submissive mind may hope to attain.

I must also add one thing more that has just flashed upon me tonight in a kind of illumination, due no doubt to the state of prayer in which, by God's

help, I have been living for some time past. It is this:
all real thought is nothing but reflected light. To
reflect, as the word shows, is to reflect God. From
which it follows that all real thought submits itself
to God. The man who believes he is thinking by himself and who turns the mirror of his mind away from
God ceases, properly speaking, to *reflect*. The highest
thought is that in which God may recognize Himself
as in a mirror.

These last truths unfortunately did not occur to
me till today; if, on the evening I have mentioned, I
could have communicated them to Éveline, I cannot
help thinking they would have had virtue enough to
convince her. Alas, how often the words we should
have said come to our minds only when it is too late!

Éveline was confined three days after that evening
which proved such a memorable one for me, as being
the occasion on which I first became aware of what
had no doubt begun long before—the rift between
Éveline and myself. I had been vaguely conscious of
it, but until then I had refused to pay any attention
to it, as I know only too well that, in the case of feelings, it is often the attention we pay them that en-
courages their growth and that those we refuse to
recognize thereby cease to exist. It is by dwelling on
subjects that should never be mentioned that many
novelists of the present day exercise such a perni-
cious influence. But it was no longer possible for me

to ignore this little rift which was soon to become a gulf—no longer possible to avoid taking it into account.

I was very busy at that time and was not in the house when Éveline's labor began. I was occupied with a new scheme, the idea of which had just occurred to me and which, thanks to my activity, turned out such a complete success that I believe it is worth while saying a few words about it here. This scheme was an offshoot of the one I have already mentioned for forming a competent jury to recommend books to the public. It struck me that the readers of these books would be delighted to be guided also in their choice of the shops in which to buy them, and that I might do the public as well as the booksellers a real service. I approached the latter, pointed out the advantage it would be to them to get into touch (on terms that I named) with an already constituted and select clientele; I also approached the publishers of the books chosen by the jury, and they agreed to insert in these volumes lists and prospectuses of the firms of booksellers deserving recommendation. This scheme, which, as I say, succeeded beyond all expectation and soon developed more extensively than I had ventured to hope, took up a considerable portion of my time and energy.

When I came in that evening, Éveline's labor had begun.

PART

ii

I WROTE the above straight on, without taking time
to revise it, and I have just become aware of a very
curious slip of my memory—or rather a mistake as
to dates. The conversation I have just related—with
great exactitude, I believe—took place, not at the
moment of Gustave's birth, but seven years later, at
the time of Éveline's third pregnancy, which, however, ended very unfortunately in a bad miscarriage.
This curious mistake of mine is no doubt due to the
damage done to my head in July 1914 by the auto
accident in which I was the victim; but it has other
causes too that lie much deeper. The present now
sheds its light over the past and I see, almost in spite
of myself, that the rift of which I have spoken
stretches back to a more remote period than I at first
realized; it no doubt existed already, though I was
as yet unable to perceive it. Moreover, I find it difficult to attach importance to the chronological de-
velopment of a soul; for a soul seems to me always
one and indivisible, necessarily consistent with itself;
I should like to keep Éveline's soul in my memory in
the form it will wear in the life to come. And just as
repentance wipes out transgression and whitens a
sinful past, so error casts its shadow behind over the

past, however blameless, unless God grants His ab-
solution—as I believe, as I know, indeed, was the
case with Éveline; for in her last moments she recog-
nized her errors and was reconciled to God in time to
partake of Holy Communion, so that I may hope by
the mercy of God to see her again in the world to come
such as she was in the first days of our union, such as
my love still holds her, for I have long ago forgiven
her all the suffering she caused me.

Another reflection that this mistake of dates has
caused me to make is the following: I have told how
Éveline thought fit to sow the seeds of freethinking
in her daughter's mind. But on further consideration
it seems to me now that it was Geneviève's rebellious
spirit, child though she still was, that contaminated
her mother's soul. Geneviève was then nine years old,
but as far back as I can remember she was in revolt.
It was she who by constantly asking questions about
one thing and another accustomed her mother to look
for and to give explanations, instead of answering
her "Why?" with "Because I say so," as is proper—
as I always did myself. I must add that Gustave, on
the contrary, from his earliest years, showed the
greatest respect and docility, accepting whatever I
said without ever questioning my words. When his
mother tried to encourage a doubting and inquiring
spirit in him, it was delightful to hear the child answer so ingenuously and yet so decidedly: "Papa
said so," just as I myself opposed the incontrovertible

instructions of the Most High's ministers to Éveline's uneasy questionings.

Astonishment may be felt that so young a child (I am speaking now of Geneviève) should have had any influence over her mother, and in fact the understanding between the two was so close and as it were pre-established that it is almost impossible to decide whether Éveline was encouraged to pursue her dangerous course by recognizing a likeness to herself in Geneviève's rebellious personality, whether it was really she who urged her daughter on, or whether it was the child who dragged her mother after her. But at any rate there can be no doubt as to the influence of my two friends Dr. Marchant and the painter Burgweilsdorf. I have already spoken of this, but I must return to the subject. So far, it has been Éveline's freethinking that I have particularly mentioned, but this was not the form her rebellion first took. No, it chose, in imitation of Burgweilsdorf, a form that was far more insidious, for it hid itself under the appearance of a virtue—namely, sincerity. This word was constantly in Burgweilsdorf's mouth; he used it as a weapon, defensively when he was accused of painting with unnecessary audacity and strangeness, and offensively too, against the teachings of tradition and authority. Not that he failed to admire certain great masters of the past and to defer to their example, as I used to point out to Éveline and himself. But he was apt to stigmatize as hypocrisy—at any rate as insin-

cerity—all striving after improvement and all sub-
ordination of feeling and emotions to an ideal. And
I admit that, taking him as an artist, the new and
peculiar accent of his painting was due to this assid-
uous search for the utmost sincerity of expression; I
admit this all the more willingly as I was one of the
first to recognize the value of his art. But by a grad-
ual shifting of ideas that soon became noticeable,
Éveline began to introduce this notion of sincerity
into the domain of morals; I do not say it is absolutely out of place there, but I do say there may be
great danger in introducing it into such questions if
it is not at the same time counterbalanced and kept
in check by a superior notion of duty. One would have
said that in Éveline's eyes it was sufficient for a feeling to be sincere for it to be praiseworthy, as if the
natural man, whom our Lord so rightly called "the
old Adam," was not the very creature that it is our
duty to combat and supplant. This is what Éveline
would no longer admit, and she refused to understand
that I could prefer in myself the person I wished to
be, the person I was trying to become, to the person
I naturally was. Without exactly accusing me of
hypocrisy, she cast suspicion on every word and act
of mine by which I endeavored to help my inward
self along the path of virtue. And as virtue was more
natural to her than to me, and as she had no bad
instincts to curb (unless it were, as I have said, a
spirit of intellectual curiosity), I could not succeed in

persuading her of the danger there might be in yielding to oneself, in accepting oneself simply for what
one was—that is to say, in short, for something really
rather worthless. I should have liked to repeat to her
an exhortation that I am grateful to Father Bredel
for pointing out to me in Fénelon's *Lettres spiri-
tuelles: "Vous avez besoin qu'on retienne les saillies
continuelles de votre imagination trop vive: tout vous
amuse, tout vous dissipe, tout vous replonge dans le
naturel!"* * And yet it was not with me that Éveline
had fallen in love, but with the man I was desirous of
being. And now she seemingly reproached me at one
and the same time for wishing to become different
from what I was and for not having perfectly succeeded.

Let me add that this worship of sincerity involves
a kind of fallacious plurality of our being, for as soon
as we abandon ourselves to our instincts, we learn all
too soon that the soul that refuses to submit to any
kind of rule necessarily becomes inconsistent and
divided. The sense of duty demands and obtains from
us that unity without which our soul can have no consciousness of itself and cannot therefore be saved.
And after that it matters little whether it feels constant and equal to itself all day and every day; it may
perhaps waver, but its waverings will be round a fixed
axis; the idea of duty steadies and focuses it. This is

* "The continual sallies of your too lively imagination need to
be controlled: you are amused by everything, dissipated by
everything, forever relapsing into the natural man!"

what I tried to make Éveline understand, but, alas, in vain.

Dr. Marchant's influence, though of another order, subtly reinforced Burgweilsdorf's in a way I hope to make clear. I one day heard him quote the saying of some celebrated doctor: "There are no illnesses—there are individuals who are ill." One can understand what the doctor and Marchant meant by this—that illness does not exist absolutely, irrespective of man, and also that every man in and through whom an illness is manifested modifies the illness, refracts it, so to speak, according to his particular humor and idiosyncrasies. But—and this to my mind is where the danger of education for women comes in—Éveline began to push this really simple, though seemingly paradoxical remark to the bounds of absurdity and to assimilate ideas to illnesses, so that she soon refused to admit of any Truth irrespective of man and considered our souls not as receptacles for holding it, but as little divinities capable of creating it. In vain I warned her of the impiety of this deification of her own person and reminded her of Satan's words: *"Et eritis sicut Dii."* Alas! Marchand's atheism encouraged her; he is, as I have said, a man of great distinction in his own line, and Éveline availed herself of his authority to consider truth in its relation to man, and not man in his relation to God.

One evening, however, I thought I was going to

regain my hold over her. The business of the jury I had founded, as related above, for the selection of the best books, had been the means of my coming into contact with an eminent philosopher and mathematician, whose name I will refrain from mentioning as he is still alive and I should be sorry to wound his modesty. I had invited him to dinner along with a few other well-known people, among whom was Dr. Marchant. After dinner the conversation turned upon questions of relativity and subjectivity, and I was not a little interested to hear the mathematician speak as follows: the world of numbers and geometrical shapes has, it is true, no existence outside the mind that creates it; but once the mathematician has created this world of his, it escapes his control and becomes obedient to laws that it is out of his power to modify, so that this man-made universe becomes one with the absolute of which man himself is a dependent part. "And this fully proves," I added, when I was left alone with Éveline after our guests had gone, "that man's mind has been created by God to know Him, just as his heart has been created by God to love Him."

But Éveline's mind was so constituted that she managed to extract from this very truth an argument for persisting in error. She had listened to X. with the liveliest interest and I could see in her face the profound impression he was making on her. But it was only the next morning that she said:

"If my reason has been given me by God, it cannot be required to obey any other laws than those God imposes on it."

A rationalist would not have argued otherwise.

"In that case," I said, "there is no need to speak of God at all."

"You are right," she answered, "there is perhaps no need." And, as a matter of fact, from that day forward she made a point of never using the word, which seemed to have lost all meaning for her.

Poor Éveline! And yet I did not cease to love her. It was to her I owed—had once owed—all the love and poetry of which I was capable. But she changed so much that I began to ask myself what it was I still loved in her. Her face lost its brightness; I looked in vain for that warmth of expression which in the early days had made my heart melt with tenderness; her voice was no longer timid; her very bearing was more self-confident. Yet she was my wife and I told myself that neither time nor she herself could alter what I loved. And so I came to understand that changes of this kind, which are sometimes marked by actual deterioration, do not after all affect the soul. It was Éveline's soul that my soul had loved and to which it was bound by indissoluble ties. But what fearful torture it is to see the woman one has chosen to be one's companion and mate for all eternity sinking daily deeper and deeper into the night of error!

"It's no use, my dear," she would say to me with what tenderness was left her, "we are not making for the same heaven."

And I would insist that there could no more be two heavens than two Gods, and that that mirage which she had taken for her goal and which she called *her heaven* could only be *my hell*—could only be hell.

All this, it is scarcely necessary to say, brought me all the nearer to God and helped me to understand the incomparable quality of His love for us and of ours for Him—for Him who alone cannot change. I remembered the words of the Apocalypse: "Happy are those who die in the Lord," and I added for my own part: "Happy are those who love in the Lord"; and as I repeated these words to myself, they grew more and more charged with melancholy longing, for this was a happiness that Éveline, alas, was never to know again.

I have told how by a curious confusion of dates I situated a certain conversation as having taken place during Éveline's second pregnancy, whereas in reality I should have set it seven years later, at a time when she had very little further to go along the road of rebellion and impiety. Her third pregnancy put her life in danger and for some days I was in a position to hope that the idea of death would restore her to a better frame of mind. Our old friend Father Bredel, who hoped so too, was all devotion. Éveline was already in her eighth month when she had an attack of influenza that resulted in the destruction of our hopes. She was prematurely delivered of a poor little stillborn child. The next day puerperal fever set in and kept her hovering for more than a week between life and death. Notwithstanding a temperature of 104°, however, she was perfectly clearheaded, and although Dr. Marchant felt confident of saving her, she was aware of her danger.

"The first condition necessary for recovery is to have faith in it," Marchant said, and with this in his mind he did all he could to hide from Éveline the extreme gravity of her condition and to encourage her in what he considered a salutary illusion.

"In cases of this kind what proportion of women recover?" I asked him.

"One in ten," he replied, and then added immediately: "but Éveline will be that tenth one," with so much authority and assurance that I felt considerably cheered. I made up my mind, however, to let Father Bredel know he might be needed. Éveline, in spite of her increasing unbelief, still kept a feeling of warm affection for Father Bredel and never set herself against him. She did not conceal from him the unfortunate direction her thoughts had taken, but as this freethinking had not led her, so far at any rate, into committing any reprehensible act, Father Bredel did not doubt she was capable of amendment and would soon recognize her error. The moment was favorable and one evening when Éveline was particularly weak and there was every reason to suppose the end at hand, I sent for the Abbé, who came bringing with him the Viaticum and Holy Oil. I spoke a few words to him in the drawing-room and was on the point of showing him into the sickroom when Marchant came out of it, shut the door behind him, and in the imperious voice he sometimes assumes forbade him to enter.

"I have just been reassuring and encouraging her," he said almost roughly. "Don't undo my work. If Éveline understands you think there is no hope, I am afraid it will be all over with her."

Father Bredel was trembling with agitation. "You have no right to prevent me from saving her soul," he murmured.

"Do you want to kill her in order to save her?" asked Marchant.

"Father Bredel is accustomed to these conversations *in extremis,*" I said by way of being conciliatory. "He will manage not to frighten Éveline; he will not suggest her receiving Communion as a dying person, but—"

Marchant interrupted me: "How long is it since she went to Communion last?"

And as the Abbé and I lowered our heads without having the courage to answer:

"You see for yourselves," he went on, "that she cannot fail to take it for a final precaution."

I took Marchant's hand. He too was trembling with agitation.

"My dear friend," said I as gently as I could, "the approach of death may greatly modify our thoughts. We have no right to let Éveline remain ignorant of the gravity of her condition. The idea that she might die without the consolations of religion is intolerable to me. She may, almost unconsciously perhaps, be expecting them—longing for them. Perhaps she is only waiting for one word—for just the last fear you wish to spare her—in order to draw near to God. How many people we know whom the fear of death—"

Marchant put all the scorn he could into the look he flung me; then, opening the door of the room himself, "Very well; go in and frighten her," he said, standing aside to let the Abbé pass.

Éveline's eyes were wide open. When she saw the Abbé, she smiled fleetingly in a way I can only call angelic.

"Ah! there you are," said she in a whisper. "I thought you would come this evening." An expression of unusual gravity came over her features as she added: "And I see you have not come alone."

Then she asked the little Sister who was nursing her to leave us.

The Abbé went up to the bed, at the foot of which I had knelt down, and stood a few moments without speaking; then, in a voice in which solemnity and tenderness mingled:

"My child," he said, "I have brought with me One who has long watched over you. He expects you to make ready to greet Him."

"Marchant has been trying to reassure me," said Éveline, "but I am not frightened. For the last two days I have been feeling ready. Robert, come nearer, dear."

I drew near without rising. Then she put her frail hand on my head and stroked it gently.

"My dear," said she, "I have sometimes had thoughts and feelings that have perhaps grieved you; and you don't know them all. I should like you to forgive me, and if now I have to leave you, I should like—"

She stopped a moment and turned her face away from me, then with a great effort went on louder and very distinctly:

"I should like you only to remember your Éveline of the early days."

As she passed her hand over my cheeks, she must have felt they were wet with tears. She herself was not crying.

"My child," then said the Abbé, "don't you feel the need of a reconciliation with God too?"

Éveline turned her face toward us again and exclaimed with a kind of sudden excitement:

"Oh, I made my peace with Him long ago!"

"But, my child," went on the Abbé, "*He* has not yet granted you His peace. That alone is not suffi-

cient for Him, nor should it be for you. The sacrament must conclude it." And leaning over her,
"Would you like Robert to leave us, you and me,
to talk alone for a few moments?" he asked.

Then Éveline: "Why? I have nothing private to
say to you. Nothing I want to hide from him."

"I understand that the faults you have to reproach
yourself with are not acts; but there are thoughts too
that we may have to repent of. Do you not feel that
you have sinned against God in your thoughts?"

"No," she said firmly. "Don't ask me to repent of
any thoughts I may have had. Such repentance would
not be sincere."

Father Bredel waited a moment. "Do you at any
rate humble yourself before Him? Do you feel ready
to appear before Him in perfect lowliness of mind and
heart?"

She did not answer.

The Abbé continued: "My child, Holy Communion
often brings us—should always bring us—a peace
that is not of this world, the peace our soul longs for
and cannot obtain alone and unaided. I bring you
the peace 'that passeth all understanding.' Will you
accept it with a humble spirit?"

And as Éveline still remained silent, "My child,"
he went on, "it is not certain that God wishes to call
you from us yet. Have no fear. The peace that Holy
Communion brings with it is so profound that even
our weakly bodies feel it, and I myself have often

seen it followed by an unhoped-for recovery. My
child, I ask you to allow God, if it be His will, to perform this miracle in you. If you believe in Him, He
who said to the dying: 'Arise and walk,' He who re-
suscitated Lazarus, may restore you too to health."

Éveline's features grew sharper; she shut her eyes
and I thought the end was near.

"You are tiring me a little," she said rather plain-
tively. "Listen, dear Father Bredel; I should be glad
to satisfy you, and I can assure you there is no feeling of revolt in my heart. I will submit. But I dislike
cheating. I don't believe in the life everlasting. If I
accept the sacrament you bring, it will be without
believing in it. It is for you to judge whether in that
case I am worthy to receive it."

Father Bredel hesitated a moment and then, "Do
you remember," he asked, "what you used to say
about your father when you were quite a child? I
will repeat the same words to you with the absolute
conviction of my soul: 'God will save you in spite
of yourself.' "

Éveline sank into a gentle sleep as soon as she had
communicated. Her hand, which I took while she was
asleep, was no longer burning, and when Marchant
came about midnight, he found an extraordinary
change for the better.

"You see I was right to be hopeful," said he, deliberately refusing, in face of the plain evidence, to ad-

mit the miraculous efficacity of the sacrament, so that the very event that should have been most convincing merely served to strengthen each one of us in his own way of thinking. And Éveline herself, who yet had plenty of time to reflect during a very long convalescence, came out of this trial without any acknowledgment of God's grace and more stubborn-minded than ever . . . like those persons who, the Scriptures point out, having eyes see not and having ears do not hear, so that I almost went so far as to regret God had not taken her to Himself when she was in a more humble frame of mind and, in the very midst of her incredulity, had nevertheless accepted Him.

I made some reflections on this subject that, as they are particularly important, I will transcribe here:

The first, which was the result of a conversation I had with Father Bredel on the day following that memorable evening, was tinged with melancholy astonishment. What! we said to each other, is it possible that death should be more terrifying to the believer than to the infidel, who has so many reasons for fearing it more? The Christian, when he is on the point of appearing before his supreme Judge, has a more agonizing consciousness of his unworthiness, and this consciousness helps toward his redemption, while at the same time it keeps him in salutary terror; while the infidel's want of a similar consciousness, as it enables him to die in a state of illusory serenity,

sets the final seal on his perdition; he withholds himself from Christ, refuses the redemption that is offered
him and of which he does not, alas, feel the urgent
necessity, so that the very calm he thinks he enjoys,
his very tranquillity in the face of death, ensure in a
measure his damnation, which is never nearer than
when he is thinking of it least.

Let me add at once that when I use that terrible
word "damnation," I am not thinking of Éveline,
who, as I have said before, was reconciled, to the best
of my belief, with God in her last moments and died,
I hope and trust, a Christian; and, indeed, she had
accepted God even at the time of this false alarm.
Nevertheless Father Bredel and myself asked ourselves whether we ought not to have frightened her
a little more at that time, instead of reassuring her
like Marchant, who was more anxious for the well-
being of her body than of her soul, failing as he did
to understand that the loss of the latter might be
brought about by the very saving of the former.

The second reflection, which I made concurrently
with Father Bredel, concerns the terrible effect of
Holy Communion when it is insufficiently desired
and, so to say, undeserved (for which among us sin-
ners ever deserves that ineffable gift?), when the soul,
as God draws near, makes no effort to draw near to
God. For then the light it has unlovingly absorbed
seems to obscure it. Certainly Éveline appeared after
this more than ever plunged in darkness. When I saw

her after her return from Arcachon, where she went
to recover—without me, for my work at that time
kept me in Paris—I felt she had set herself more
resolutely than ever against every good influence,
against every word of advice I tried to give her. In
the lines of her forehead, in the double vertical bar
that was beginning to show between her eyebrows, I
could read her growing obstinacy, her antagonism not
only to the sacred truths of religion, but to everything
I could say to her, to everything that came from me.
The ironical scrutiny of her look made my most meritorious actions appear in some way constrained, designed, affected. Or rather her scrutiny acted on me
like a surgeon's knife, severing such or such a word
or gesture or action from me so sharply that it seemed
like an alien thing I had adopted rather than a real
part of myself. Far from being able to pray with her
and lift up both our hearts together toward God as
I should have liked, I soon became afraid of praying
in her presence, or if the hope of carrying her soul
along with mine induced me to persist, my prayer,
even though it remained unformulated, would at once
lose its power of ascension and, like the smoke of an
unaccepted sacrifice, drop miserably back to earth.
In the same way, if I stretched out my hand to give
alms, her smile incontinently withered up my heart,
and it was thanks to her that this action of mine, in
which my heart no longer had a share, resembled the
behavior of the Pharisee in the Gospel, so that I no

longer felt that profound joy which is the heart's chief
recompense for charity.

I have said that Éveline's growing unbelief rooted
me all the more strongly in my religious convictions,
in my faith. But what I refuse to admit is that my
virtue, imperfect though it may be, had anything to
do with destroying her faith, as she gives it to be
understood in her journal. I repudiate this dreadful
accusation, which is intended to throw the responsibility for her deleterious opinions upon me. A believer, however blundering, is still a believer, and
even though he sing the praises of God with an un-
tuneful voice, it is not for that that God will mis-
judge him, nor should His image on that account be
distorted in the minds of others.

I do not, however, wish to blame Éveline too severely; I do as a fact believe her nature was funda-
mentally better than mine; but was that a reason why
every movement of my soul that was not absolutely
spontaneous should be accounted insincere? Éveline
was naturally virtuous; I strove after virtue. But is
not that the duty of us all? Was I wrong not to accept
myself as I was, to wish myself to be better? Without
such constant striving what would a man be worth?
Is not each of us, when he is abandoned to himself, a
miserable sinner? What Éveline despised in me was
my effort after improvement—the only thing about
me that was not despicable. No doubt she had mistaken me at first, but how could I help that? In the

early days, her love blinded her to my failings, my inadequacies; but was it right of her to bear me a grudge later on if I was less intelligent, less kind, less virtuous, less courageous than she had at first imagined me? The more I felt my shortcomings, the greater need I had of her love. I have always thought that "great men" have not so much need of love as we. And was not my effort to resemble the man she once took me for—the man who was better than I—was not my perseverance, my zeal, particularly deserving of her love?

The fresh experience I have made—with God's counsel and aid—since Éveline's death has been a conclusive proof of the help that married love may be to us here below. What might I not have done with my life if I had been a little better understood, supported, encouraged by my first wife! But it seemed that her one anxiety on the contrary was to bring me back, to lower me down to the level of the natural man whom it was my endeavor to surpass. As I have said, the only thing she cared for in me was that "old Adam" from whom our Lord came to deliver us.

Poor Éveline! She aspired after no heaven. How could she have helped me to reach that divine home which religion enables us, even here below, to have a glimpse of? How could I hope ever to meet her there? It was this consideration that, with the help of Providence, induced me to marry again, after a decent period of widowhood. For God consented to look with indulgence on the great need I felt of gaining a companion for the short time that remains to me on earth, and also for the life everlasting, if so be that God, who must then fill our hearts, does not absorb all love into Himself.

GENEVIÈVE

or

THE UNFINISHED CONFIDENCE

Shortly after the publication in the Revue de Paris *of* The School for Wives *and its sequel,* Robert, *I received, in manuscript, the first portion of a tale that was in some sort complementary to them; that is to say that, taken in conjunction with the other two, it might be looked upon as the third panel of a triptych. After having long waited for its continuation, I have decided to print this beginning as it stands, with the letter that accompanied it to serve as introduction.*

ANDRÉ GIDE

August 1931

S<small>IR</small>:

May I hope that you will consent to lend the cover of your name to the book I am sending you herewith, as you did before for my mother's journal and my father's answer to it?

I am afraid that this book will not be at all to your liking. Not being particularly drawn toward literature, I confess that I have not read much of your work—enough, however, to be pretty certain that the questions that interest me are a matter of indifference to you. At any rate, I find no trace of them in your books. The subjects you treat of are as far removed as possible from what you seem to consider as "contingences" unworthy of your attention, whereas here you will find nothing but problems of a practical nature set down without any attempt at art. Your mind soars aloft in the absolute, while I am wrestling with the relative. The question for me is not, as it is for the heroes you depict and for yourself, in a vague and general way, *what is it possible for man to do?* but in a perfectly material and definite way: what

147

may a woman of the present day actually expect and hope for?

Is it not natural that this "problem" should seem to a woman who is still young like myself of primal importance? But important as it is, it is only in our own time that it has actually come to the fore. Yes, it is only since the war, during which so many women proved themselves more valuable and more energetic than men had thought possible, that people have begun to recognize and they themselves have begun to lay claim to virtues that are not purely negative, such as devotion, submission, and fidelity—devotion to men, submission to men, fidelity to men—for up to the present time all the positive virtues had seemed to be the particular birthright of men, and men had exclusively reserved them to themselves. No one, I think, can dispute today that the position of women has considerably changed since the war. And perhaps nothing less than that appalling catastrophe was needed to enable women to make proof of qualities that up to then had seemed exceptional—to enable the value of women to be taken into serious consideration.

My mother's book was addressed to an earlier generation. In my mother's youth a woman might wish for liberty; at the present time it is not a matter of wishing for liberty, but of taking it. How and for what ends? This is what is important and this is what I want to try to speak of, at any rate as regards myself.

I am certainly not setting myself up as an example, but it seems to me that the simple story of my life which I am telling here may serve as a warning; I give it as a sequel to my mother's journal, as a *New School for Women*. And in order to make it clear that it is only one example among many—only an individual example—I will call it *Geneviève,* the assumed name under which I already figure in my mother's journal.

PART

i

In 1913, when I was just turned fifteen, my mother sent me to the *lycée* as a day scholar, in spite of my father's disapproval; but my father, who notwithstanding his masterful airs was weak-willed, used invariably to give in, and consoled himself by paying off his score with the small change of incessant criticism. My school education, according to him, was responsible for my "errors of thought," and later for my "errors of conduct."

I have inherited from my mother a considerable liking for work and a naturally diligent disposition, which she encouraged by pretending to continue her own education alongside of mine. When I came back from school, she helped me with my home preparation and learned my lessons with me. I used to tell her everything I learned in class just as other people might tell what they have seen or heard during a trip to town. This, I suppose, is what gave her the illusion that I had more influence over her than she had over me. She endeavored to convey this illusion (if it was one) to me too, and nothing could have helped me more to mature, to keep alive my zeal and inspire me with the self-confidence in which she herself was lacking.

I owe my mother too an ardent desire to make myself useful, and if this desire was already innate in
me—although dormant—she succeeded in arousing
and quickening it. In my mother it was fed by an
extraordinary love of the poor, of the suffering, of
all those my father used to call (my mother never
would) "the lower classes." I am all the more anxious
to say this as neither my mother's journal nor my
father's answer breathe a word of it. It was not only
without ostentation that my mother wore herself out
in her devotion to others, but with a constant endeavor to keep her labors concealed, as indeed everything else that might have brought her credit. This
extreme modesty and self-effacement (which I freely
confess I have not inherited from her) were such that
it was possible to live beside her for years without suspecting her virtues. My father, on the contrary, was
as constantly anxious to show himself off as my
mother to efface herself. He seemed to attach more
value to the appearance of virtue than to virtue itself.
I don't think he was exactly a hypocrite or that he
made no effort to become what he pretended to be;
but his words and actions preceded his emotions and
thoughts, so that he was always in arrears, in debt,
as it were, to himself. My mother suffered from this
greatly, and I loved her too much not to detest my
father.

In class, the girl who sat on my right was the one

of all my schoolfellows whose appearance most attracted me. Her complexion was dark, and her black, curly, almost frizzy hair hid her temples and part of her forehead. She couldn't have been called exactly beautiful, but her strange charm appealed to me much more than beauty. Her name was Sara and she was very particular about having it spelled without an "h." When a little later I read Victor Hugo's *Orientales*, it was of her I thought as *"belle d'indolence,"* swinging in the hammock. She dressed oddly and the cut of her bodice, open at the throat, showed a bust that was already formed. Her hands, seldom clean and with bitten fingernails, were extraordinarily slender.

"Why on earth do you keep staring at me like that?" she asked me suddenly the first day of term.

I looked away blushing, without daring to tell her that it was because I thought her charming. The other girls did not seem to share my opinion, and I overheard them criticizing her "gypsy" complexion. Her serious expression and the slight but almost continual frowning of her brows seemed to show a singular tension of spirit, a fixed attention to—what? I should have liked to know, for it was certainly not to her lessons. When it was her turn to be questioned, it became obvious that she had not been listening; and if in her moments of tension she looked older than any of the rest of us (though she told me that she was exactly my own age), a minute later a sudden fit of joy, a kind of ecstasy of merriment, would plunge her back again into childhood.

At the very beginning I fell into a confused medley of feelings for her which I had never experienced for anyone else, and which seemed to me so new, so peculiar, that I wondered whether it was really I, Geneviève, who was feeling it or whether it was not the personality of some stranger who had ousted me from the possession of my mind and body. Sara, however, appeared barely to notice me and there was scarcely any extravagance I did not feel capable of committing in order to attract her attention. I tried to imagine what might give her pleasure; she seemed indifferent unfortunately to any school successes and I was piqued to see how little she noticed mine. When I spoke to her, she barely answered; nothing I said ever seemed to interest her. She was certainly far from being stupid and her prestige was so great in my eyes that I felt convinced there was some point in which she must shine; but I could not discover in what. One day when we were having a recitation lesson, I had a sudden revelation. After several girls and I myself had jogged more or less laboriously through our stock pieces—the Cid's stanzas, Athalie's dream, Théramène's proverbial speech—with no care except not to stumble, and as if this poetry had been written with no end in view but to exercise our memory, our French mistress called upon Sara:

"Come here, up to my desk, and show us how poetry ought to be recited."

Sara, without the least embarrassment, went forward and, facing the class, began to repeat the first scene of *Britannicus*. Her voice, fuller and deeper than usual, took on a sonority I had never heard in it before. Like the rest of the class, I had learned these lines by heart; our teacher had commented upon them and pointed out their excellence, but I had never before perceived their beauty. Sara's recitation suddenly revealed it to me; a kind of religious thrill ran down my spine and shook me to my depths, while my eyes filled with tears. Our mistress herself seemed moved.

"Thank you, Mademoiselle Keller," she said at last, after the recitation was finished, "we all thank you. With your gifts it is inexcusable that you shouldn't work more."

Sara made an ironical little curtsy, a sort of pirouette, and returned to her place beside me.

I was quivering with an admiration, with an enthusiasm I longed to express, but there came to my mind only words that I was afraid she would think ridiculous. The lesson was nearly over. I quickly tore a piece off the foot of one of the pages of my copybook, scribbled on it with a trembling hand: "I should like to be friends with you," and slipped this note awkwardly toward her.

I saw her crumple the paper up and roll it between her fingers. I hoped for a glance, a smile, from her, but her face remained impassive and more impenetrable than ever. I felt I could not endure her disdain and made ready to hate her.

"Tear that thing up," I said in a choking voice. But she suddenly unfolded the paper again, passed her hand over it to smooth it out, and as though she had come to a decision— At that moment I heard my name: the teacher was calling me. I had to stand up, and I mechanically recited a short poem of Victor Hugo's, which I luckily knew very well. As soon as I sat down again, Sara slipped the note into my hand again; on the back of it she had written: "Come and see us next Sunday at 3 o'clock." My heart swelled with pleasure and I boldly said:

"But I don't know where you live."

Then she: "Pass me the paper."

And as the lesson had come to an end and the girls were collecting their things and getting up to leave, she wrote at the bottom of the note:

"Sara Keller, 16 rue Campagne-Première."

"I don't know whether I shall be able to," I said prudently. "I must ask Mother."

She did not exactly smile, but just raised the corners of her lips. She might have been laughing at me, and I added quickly:

"I'm afraid we may be invited somewhere already."

Living as I did in another section and some way from the school, I had to part from Sara as soon as we came out. I generally walked back alone and very quickly. My mother wanted to show her confidence in me by not coming for me, but she had made me promise always to go straight home and not stay talking to the other girls. That day, such was my hurry to tell her about Sara's invitation, that I ran most of the way back. I was not at all sure my mother would allow me to accept it, for she very rarely let me go out alone except to school. As a rule I had no secrets from my mother, but some odd feeling of reserve had so far prevented me from speaking to her about Sara. I had to pour it all out at once—the recitation of *Britannicus,* and my enthusiasm, which I didn't attempt to conceal, and even that strange attraction, which I was incapable of hiding and which, in spite of myself, was obvious in every word of my tale. When at last I asked: "May I go?" my mother didn't answer at once. I knew she was always sorry to refuse me anything.

"First of all, I should like to know a little more about your new friend and about her parents. Did you ask her what her father did?"

I admitted I hadn't thought of that and promised to find out. There were still two more days before Sunday.

"I'll come and get you tomorrow when you come out of school," added my mother; "you must try to introduce me to this girl; I should like to know her."

That Saturday I looked at Sara attentively, wondering anxiously what my mother would think of her. It seemed to me she was more carelessly dressed than usual; her hair in particular was very untidy.

"Do tidy your hair a little," I said at last rather timidly.

"Why?"

"Because Mamma's coming for me. She wants to know you."

"Yes; before she decides whether she should let you come on Sunday, I suppose."

I couldn't deny it, and yet I didn't want to seem too much under my mother's thumb.

"Perhaps," I said. "Oh, I do so want her to like you!" I stopped myself from adding: "and you to like her," but I began to ask myself anxiously what dress and what hat my mother would be wearing.

"I don't much care for this examination," said Sara.

Nevertheless, when we came out of school, she did not try to avoid the meeting, as I was afraid she might. Mamma was at the door. I think she herself was anxious to please my friend; she looked more charming, I thought, than I had ever seen her.

"I have heard a great deal about you from Geneviève," she said to Sara with the sweetest kindness. "I should have liked to hear you recite those lines of Racine's. They are so fine. . . . But I think you couldn't have said them so well if you hadn't liked them."

She was obviously trying to find something that would encourage Sara to talk. And Sara was certainly far less agitated than I was.

"Oh yes," she answered at once; "but I should have preferred reciting something of Baudelaire's."

I had never read anything by Baudelaire and was afraid Mamma didn't know much about him either; would she show it?

"What, for instance?"

"Oh, 'The Death of Lovers' for choice."

I felt myself blushing. Surely my mother would be shocked by this title. I looked at her. She was smiling.

"But no doubt it's not the right kind of poetry for the *lycée*," she said. "Have you any brothers and sisters?"

"An older brother who is doing his military service in Algeria"; then, as if forestalling a question of my mother's: "My father's a painter."

"What!" cried Mamma. "Are you the daughter of the Alfred Keller whose pictures were so much admired in the last Salon? That explains your artistic tastes."

I was delighted to learn that Sara's father was celebrated; but suddenly a shade came over my mother's face and, to my consternation, she added: "I know you have invited Geneviève for next Sunday; unfortunately she won't be free."

And as Sara replied rather stiffly: "I'm sorry," my mother held out her hand, saying: "It'll be for another time."

"But you never told me," said my mother as soon as Sara had left us, "that she was a Jewess."

This word had practically no meaning for me. I had learned Bible History and knew about the Jews in ancient times, but nothing whatever about them at the present day. An almost imperceptible shade in her tone of voice had wounded me painfully.

"A Jewess?" I cried. "How do you know?"

"One has only to look at her. But she's very pretty, all the same." And then, as if she were following two ideas at the same time, "For that matter," she said, "there are a great many Jews at the *lycée*."

"Is that," I ventured to ask, "why you won't let me go to see her? Why did you say I wasn't free? You know quite well it isn't true."

"My dear, I couldn't tell her brutally that we refused her invitation. It's not her fault that she's a Jew and her father an artist. I didn't want to hurt her. And besides," she added, seeing my eyes full of tears, "the Jews have many excellent qualities, and some of them are very remarkable. But I had rather not let you go into a set so different from ours without knowing a little more about them."

"Oh, Mamma, I did so want to—"

"Not this time, my child. Don't insist. In any case, it's too late now." And then, more tenderly: "Come, Geneviève, you know how sorry I am to hurt you."

Yes, I did know; but my mother's refusal seemed to me to be caused by worldly considerations, coming less from her own self than from our connections, our position, our social rank; I felt this vaguely; and as a rule she taught me not to take such things as these into account. It was perfectly natural, however, that she should not let me, so young and still so impressionable, associate with people whom she didn't know and who were perhaps undesirable. I felt this vaguely too; and in my heart no doubt I approved her decision. But it seemed to me I was being separated from my new friend by an artificially raised barrier of conventions and it made me extremely unhappy.

"Still," my mother went on after a long silence, "I don't want to prevent you from seeing your schoolfellow; perhaps you might even invite her to come to our house. We'll see about it later."

Certainly she was very sorry to have to cause me this pain; it seemed as though she was almost trying to excuse herself and doing her best to console me. But a little later a still worse pain was added to the first.

I saw Sara again the following Monday.

"It's a pity your mother didn't let you come yesterday," she began at once. Then with a kind of cruelty, and as if it amused her to mingle with my natural regrets the bitter poison of jealousy, "Gisèle was there," she went on. "Father took us to the Palais de Glace. Gisèle sprained her ankle. That's why she couldn't come to school this morning. But we had tremendous fun."

Gisèle Parmentier was the cleverest girl in our class. Her father, who had died long before, had been, I was told, a distinguished professor at the Collège de

France. Her mother was English. Gisèle, her only child, spoke English as well as French. She was more intelligent than clever. It seemed to cost her no effort to keep at the head of all the other girls in the school. But it was still more her friendship with Sara that made me notice her. They used to have long conversations together, and Sara did not talk much to anyone else. Gisèle, on the contrary, was very much sought after in the recesses and seemed to pay no attention to me—"the new girl." She sat at the other end of the room and I could only get near her during the minutes of recess, when the girls were free to scatter about as they pleased in the playground—a big square planted with trees. One day, as I came up to an extremely animated group clustered around Gisèle, one of the girls turned abruptly toward me and asked me my opinion on some rather ticklish subject (I've forgotten what) on which, it seemed, they couldn't agree; and as I didn't answer immediately, another girl exclaimed: "Oh, Miss Geneviève is far too well brought up to take sides! She'd be afraid of compromising herself."

This attack seemed to me highly unjust. I at once felt I was capable of doing anything to prove to Gisèle that I deserved the esteem which apparently was refused me; to prove to her, and to myself, that the fear of compromising myself would never stop me, in spite of my reserved manners and my appearance of being "too well brought up." Capable of doing—but exactly what? That I didn't know.

I shrugged my shoulders and muttered: "Those who talk most aren't always—"

"What is she saying? What is she saying?" several of them cried out confusedly.

"—aren't always those who do most."

I had no sooner said these words than they seemed absurd. Fortunately no one took them up.

When Sara told me that Gisèle had sprained her ankle, I felt a spiteful pleasure. A few days' respite, I thought. Gisèle and Sara were the only two of all the girls with whom I wanted to make friends. Looked down upon by the former and obliged by my mother to refuse the latter's advances, I felt my solitude bitterly and went about plunged in melancholy, when one day my mother, who of course noticed my gloom, told me that she had persuaded my father to write to Sara's father and invite him to come with his daughter to one of our Thursday evenings.

My mother did not have an "at home" day and even professed an aversion to society duties—an attitude with which my father never ceased to reproach her. He considered her responsible for his failures; for, like all those whose personal value is not very great, he liked to believe that everything in this world is obtained by means of intrigue or social connections. I think that the chief part of what he pompously called his "work" consisted in paying his respects to other people and receiving like attentions from them, of which transactions he kept a strict account. I quite

understand that my mother would not stoop to such
practices, which, she said, were blunting to the conscience and to that intellectual and moral honesty
which she hoped would always be mine. I have no reason to refrain from judging my father even more severely than she herself does in her journal. I consider
that nothing more completely warps a child's character than imposing on him an obligation to honor his
parents, if they do not deserve honor. My mother, on
the other hand, was worthy of all the respect and admiration I felt for her, and my love was little short of
worship. As for my father, I soon ceased to take him
seriously. No doubt these reflections were not those of
the child I then was. But it already irritated me to
hear him contradict himself, uphold opinions that I
knew were not his own, parade sublime sentiments
that he was incapable of feeling, or make sweeping
statements that thinly disguised the extreme weakness
and shallowness of his character. He called his little
moral delinquences worldly wisdom, and was very
clever at attributing all his setbacks to his fastidious-
ness, his "excessive" honesty, and his scruples, and
this so ingeniously and ingenuously that my poor
mother was driven to exasperation. But she has described all this much better than I can and there is
nothing I can really add.

How many readers will be indignant to hear me
speak so freely of my father! It is not for them I write,
and I am determined to brush aside all considerations

of so-called propriety, decency, or self-respect. The whole point of my story is its perfect frankness, and if this frankness sometimes takes on the color of cynicism, I believe that it is because of the inveterate habit people have of looking askance at, or altogether avoiding, or approaching only by way of reassuring circumlocutions certain subjects that I intend to look squarely in the face, as they should be looked at.

I believe (but I am now speaking of my more mature reflections)—I believe more and more firmly that there are very few of our ills that are not due to ignorance, and that their remedy can only be found by first casting on them a full and seaching light. Considerations of delicacy and morality are here out of place; they merely tend to falsify every problem. And there are some we still approach with a paralyzing reserve, like the modesty that so long prevented the progress of medicine and all exact anatomical knowledge by considering the examination of the human body indecent and criminal.

A careful scrutiny of the actual present ought to precede all progress toward the possible future, toward all reforms and improvements, as much of society as of the individual. This is not a novel I am writing and I shall without compunction allow myself to digress into reflections that will interrupt my story, but that, I confess, seem to me much more important than the story itself. I am relating my experience of life only in the hope that it may be of some service or help to others. I shall therefore not refrain from commentaries, even if they interfere with the "artistic quality" of these pages. I have already said I had no great taste for literature. It seems to me even that a certain degree of perfection (which I have no desire to achieve) can be obtained only at the expense of truth. Truth, as soon as it is a matter not of abstraction but of life, is always complex, confused, indistinct, and ill-adapted to definition—for which, moreover, I have no talent. It matters little if what I am writing here has no more than a passing interest. I have no intention, nor any illusion, of setting down anything eternal, and if what tormented me in the past and preoccupies me at present soon ceases to be of the smallest interest to anybody, I shall be glad of it.

This takes us a long way, M. Gide, from the considerations that inspire your works. You used to say, I remember: "I write to be reread." I, on the contrary, am writing this in order to help those (him or her) who read me to go beyond it. Everything that aids progress, everything that can help man to rise a little above his present condition should soon be pushed away as the foot pushes away the step of the ladder on which it has first been planted.

Once a week my father used to invite to dinner a few important people whose favor he wished to se-

cure. On those evenings I would go to dine with our
Froberville cousins. The next morning our lunch was
furnished with the remains of last evening's feast and
with the echoes of the table-talk. My father on these
occasions seemed more than ever penetrated with the
sense of his own importance.

Besides these dinner-parties, we used every Thursday even to be at home to a few faithful friends,
among whom were Dr. Marchant and his wife, who, I
realized, were more my mother's friends than my father's. The question arose, my mother told me afterward, whether Sara's father should be invited to one
of the full-dress dinners or to one of the quiet
evenings. He would be more impressed by the former,
but who could be invited to meet this newcomer?
. . . For Papa was terribly afraid that Keller "might
not show to advantage." Papa liked to profess great
liberal-mindedness—a pure affectation, for in reality
he was strongly anchored to all that was most conventional. He was fond of saying to anyone who would
listen that talent covers all things; but with no talent
himself, he excused nothing, and nothing distressed
him more than what he called "want of knowledge of
the world," for he had hardly any other sort of knowledge himself. Moreover, though he was not a declared
anti-Semite, he had a suspicion of all Jews. To admit
Keller to one of our quiet evenings would commit him
to nothing; and in reality the only object of the invitation was to throw Sara and me together, in spite

of my father's unconcealed dislike to seeing his daughter make friends with someone who was not "in our set."

My father congratulated himself on his decision when Keller notified us that he "never went anywhere without his wife." Mme Keller therefore was to come with Sara.

This evening which I had promised myself would be so happy was an unspeakable disappointment. It was clear, even to my childish eyes, and from the minute our new guests entered our bourgeois drawing-room, that they were completely out of place. It was not till long after that I learned (and my parents learned) that Keller was not legally married and that Sara's mother, who was of very low origin (like himself), had been his model before becoming his companion. To hear my father talk, "to marry one's model" was the lowest depths of ignominy, and yet his scorn increased when he learned that Keller had "not even married her." We knew nothing of this at the time, however, or, my father declared later, "we should naturally not have invited them." I also learned, later still, that the couple were extremely united; but that, said my father when he heard it, "makes no sort of difference." Mme Keller must have been very handsome; she was still so, though grown unfortunately stout. Her dress, which was too showy, too gorgeous, for our colorless surroundings—"extravagant" my father called it next morning—served

to throw into relief Mme Marchant's and my mother's inconspicuous modesty. But the contrast at once
made me think their dark, high-necked dresses old-
fashioned, dowdy, dull, and terribly *"comme il faut."*
As for me, that evening I was in a light dress, but it
was of extreme simplicity and I felt painfully stiff and
self-conscious when I saw Sara, who was draped har-
moniously and as if carelessly in a soft, dark-red silk,
of which the warm tint showed up the amber brightness of her skin. Not that I attached much importance
to dress, but at sight of Sara's grace and ease, and as a
result of my extreme sympathy, I was able to look
with her eyes at our home and saw revealed the insig-
nificance and banal conventionality of the surroundings in which until then I had passed my life. The
chandelier, the wallpapers, the armchairs, the furniture, all were suddenly by disenchantment turned
commonplace and dull. Not, however, that our
drawing-room was particularly unpleasing; neither
my mother nor even my father had what is known as
"bad taste," but they both sacrificed to custom; the
very propriety of the bourgeois fashion that satisfied
them, how mediocre and stupidy unenterprising it was
made to appear by Mme Keller's and Sara's style of
dress!

"Well, you *have* made yourselves comfortable!"
Sara said to me; and these were the first words she
uttered to me in an indefinable tone of voice that was
a mixture of astonished admiration combined with a

touch of irony, which seemed to me slightly contemp-
tuous and which made me blush.

My father, who had made inquiries, had told us
that Keller sold his pictures very easily and for very
high prices. But when, a little later, I visited the
studio of my friend's father, I saw nothing in particular that showed any signs of wealth. Whereas with
us everything, on the contrary, seemed designed to
proclaim indiscreetly the figure of our income.

It was impossible for me to doubt that the Kellers
made a bad impression on my parents; child as I still
was, it was only too obvious to me; but so too was the
great effort that they made not to show it. Everyone
that evening made a point of appearing perfectly at
ease and I really think I was the only one to suffer
from the discordance—no doubt because of the sincerity of my feeling for Sara. I had immediately led
her aside while our parents were taking as a pretext
for conversation some of the pictures hanging on the
walls. They were for the most part the works of our
friend Bourgweilsdorf, which my father had taken
out of his cupboards after the painter's recent death,
the dealers and the public having at that moment become suddenly aware of their value. For that matter,
my father, who was at the time busying himself with
an art review, had greatly contributed (according to
himself) to "launching" him and obtaining for him
posthumously the glory that had been withheld during the artist's lifetime.

"You know," Sara said to me, "Father pretends to like it, but in reality he detests that style of painting."

"And you?" I asked timidly.

"Oh, I! Painting doesn't interest me. I see too much of it. I only like music and poetry."

I was extremely anxious to think "well" of my friend's parents; but how vulgar I thought Mme Keller looked beside my mother and Mme Marchant! She laughed too loudly, and about everything, flinging back her head and exploding behind a large outspread fan. Later on I came to recognize she was an excellent woman, though rather foolish and unfathomably ignorant. As for Keller, I don't know how he could be at once so like his daughter and so ugly. I cannot remember any of the remarks he gave vent to with great assurance, but I well remember Dr. Marchant's very obvious irritation.

When the refreshments were brought in, Marchant profited by the interruption to ask Sara whether she wouldn't recite us something.

"Geneviève has told us of your extraordinary talent," he said. "I think some of us here would appreciate your recitation a good deal better than your schoolfellows could."

Sara needed no pressing; but as she hesitated and asked what we should like to hear, my mother said encouragingly: "Why not 'The Death of Lovers,' which you told me the other day you liked especially?"

"One of the high-water marks of French poetry," said my father sententiously. "Would you like the book, mademoiselle?"

Then he added that Baudelaire was his favorite poet and that he always kept a copy of *Les Fleurs du mal* beside him. At the same time he pulled out of a small revolving bookcase a volume whose binding he no doubt wanted people to admire, for he must have known that Sara would recite by heart. She stood with her back against the grand piano, and over her face came an expression in which sadness and smiles seemed blended and which made her more beautiful than ever. She recited in a quiet voice that was full but extraordinarily soft and melting that wonderful poem, which I then heard for the first time. I am not, I admit, very easily touched by poetry and I should have no doubt remained indifferent to these lines if I had read them to myself. But as recited by Sara, they penetrated my heart. The words lost their definite meaning, which I hardly tried to understand; each one was turned to music, and at their mysterious call there rose in my mind the vision of a sleeping paradise; I had the sudden revelation of another world, of which the outer world was only a dim and dreary reflection.

"Sara," I said to her afterward, "this world of poetry, beautiful as it is, is not the one in which we live and move. Why give us the longing for it?"

"We can live in it if we choose," she answered.

I learned that same evening that Sara intended to go on the stage. Later on, as my story will tell, I saw her gradually allowing herself to be inhabited, to be taken possession of, by all manner of borrowed personalities, to such an extent that she came to lose her own individuality. I think today that it is not a good thing (I was going to say a right thing) to give up dwelling among the miseries of this world, like certain mystics who live in the dream of a future life; and this escape from reality seems to me like a kind of desertion. But that evening I did not attempt to resist; I abandoned myself to the charm of Sara's voice as to an incantation.

Sara, at my father's request, recited also *"I'Invitation au voyage"* and *"Le Jet d'eau."* I was agreeably astonished to hear him let fall one or two remarks about Baudelaire that I thought amazing—other people's opinions, no doubt, which as usual he adopted as his own.

"That girl," said Father next day," is already an actress. Actors are all very well on the stage. But I don't like to see you associating with people of that kind." He did not dare, however, forbid me to accept the Kellers' invitation which was the natural answer to ours.

"That's what comes of having them here," said he. "Now we can't refuse."

My father, always a stickler for etiquette, thought it indecorous not to fulfill what he considered social duties. But any he disliked too much he shunted on to my mother; so that he added:

"You can go by yourselves. I shall have another engagement."

This was exactly what I wanted.

The party at the Kellers' was a large one. When we entered the studio, we were introduced to a dozen or so people—artists and writers for the most part. I found the atmosphere of the vast, queerly decorated room very disconcerting; so, no doubt, did my mother, for she told me next day that she had felt "rather lost" and that decidedly she didn't want to be on terms of closer intercourse with my friend's parents. She didn't like their "style." Notwithstanding my mother's great liberal-mindedness, she was always extremely particular.

"And yet," she added, "your friend seems to me charming, and I don't want to prevent you from seeing her. She is certainly intelligent and highly talented. But her talents seem to me so different from yours that I should be very much surprised if you were to get on together for long. You will not be able to follow where she goes, and if you become attached to her, it will be a cause of grief to you later on. That other girl—what is she called?—seems to me much more likely to suit you."

The other girl was Gisèle Parmentier, whom for so long it had made me unhappy not to be more intimate

with. I have already said that her only friend was
Sara. And I couldn't have said which of the two I was
jealous of, equally in love as I was with both of them,
though in very different ways. With Gisèle there was
no question of physical attraction as there was with
Sara, but of something deep and indefinable. No, it
was their friendship I was jealous of. That evening,
thrown together with them for the first time, I felt like
an awkward outsider and found nothing to say,
though my heart was overflowing. I hoped Sara would
recite, but a girl who was hardly older than we were
went up to the piano and began to sing to her own
accompaniment. Sara then drew Gisèle and me into
another room, which was empty and separated from
the studio by a portiere.

"My parents have asked her to sing," said she, "in
the hopes of getting her some pupils. She earns her
living by giving piano and singing lessons. But I can't
bear her voice or her manner of playing. No more can
Father really; but he's so kind. . . . And you?" she
added, turning to me. "Are you kind?"

It seemed rash to answer yes. And besides I had no
idea whether I was "kind" or not. Fortunately she did
not wait for my answer, but went on:

"As for Gisèle, she tries to love everybody. But I
say that isn't love; it's what Vedel" (one of our pro-
fessors) "calls *philanthropy*."

"No, I don't try," protested Gisèle. "But Mamma
always says—"

"Oh, Madame Parmentier," interrupted Sara, "is kindness itself. Every time one runs down anyone before her, she sticks up for them and will do nothing but find excuses for them. Well, what does your mother say?"

"That there are many more nice people than one thinks, and to like them better you've often only got to understand them better, and to understand them better, you've only got to observe them better."

Gisèle uttered this maxim without the slightest affectation, but with charming seriousness. I felt that if I didn't say something at once, I should be condemned to silence for the rest of the evening. The sound of my own voice terrified me beforehand; I felt it choking me, and it was with a great effort that I brought out:

"I don't think I'm naturally kind, but I think I'm capable of loving very much."

I wanted to add that I thought love must be all the stronger the more exclusive it was and the least spread over everybody. I wanted especially to convey that when I spoke of loving a few people, I meant to include Gisèle and Sara. But how could I put it without seeming affected? This declaration which I longed to make and which stuck in my throat made me blush as if I had made it. Gisèle and Sara looked at me; but as I could not extract another word, Sara went on:

"There are a great many ways of loving. For instance, I don't think I have any vocation for conjugal love."

"What can you know about it?" said Gisèle. "The day you meet—"

Sara interrupted her again:

"Oh, I don't mean to say I shall never fall in love with a man. But as for sacrificing my tastes, my own life, to him, thinking of nothing but being agreeable to him, waiting on him—"

"What a funny idea you have of marriage!"

"No, it isn't; it's nearly always like that, I assure you. Once married, you have no time for anything that interested you before. No time for anything but housekeeping, and looking after the children if you've got any. Look at Emily N—" (the elder sister of one of our schoolfellows); "she used to live for nothing but music. She got the first prize at the Conservatoire. Since she's married, she's never once opened her piano."

"Well, she couldn't take it with her on her honeymoon."

"No, no; she told me so; she told Mother too; she's given it up for good; and she said she'd got a great deal too much to do now; and she didn't want to improve in an art that separated her from her husband. Those are her very words."

"She ought to have married a musician," I ventured. And this time the silliness of my remark made me blush again.

"It's more prudent not to marry anyone," answered Sara.

And as I went on that it couldn't be much fun to live all alone, "One doesn't necessarily live alone," she answered.

I should not have noticed this remark, no doubt, if Gisèle had not uttered an exclamation, so that Sara retorted:

"As if you didn't agree with me! It's only because of Geneviève that you object."

Then, without understanding or realizing what I was committing myself to, and out of an immense desire to show my sympathy and not be considered an outsider, I cried:

"But *I* agree with Sara too. You mustn't be afraid of me; I can't express myself very well, because up to now I've never talked to anyone; but if you knew me better, you'd understand that I can be your friend."

I brought all this out at one blow, with an immense effort. Astonished and abashed at what I had just dared to say, with a beating heart, I seized Gisèle's hand and pressed my forehead against Sara's shoulder as though to hide my confusion. I felt Gisèle's other hand gently stroking my hair. When I raised my head, I was in tears, but managed somehow to smile.

"All right," said Sara; "in that case, we might form a league, the three of us—a secret league—the League for the Independence of Women. We must begin by promising not to speak of it to anyone. Gisèle, swear at once you won't tell your mother."

"But what could I tell her? There's nothing whatever to tell."

"What do you mean, 'nothing'? Do you call it nothing that we have joined together and promised solemnly to be faithful to our program?"

"But what program?"

"We'll draw that up later. But first of all we must swear not to tell anyone."

Until then I had never had any secrets from my mother, but I agreed that this should be the first.

"Only," said I, "before swearing, I should like to know what it binds one to."

I was laughing now and beginning to feel perfectly at my ease.

"Our league," said Sara, "shall be called the I.F.— the initials of *Indépendance Féminine*. Our emblem shall be a sprig of yew" (*if* in French). As we are the founders, no one shall become a member of the I.F. without the consent of us three. New members shall pay a subscription."

"What for?" asked Gisèle.

"To be prepared for emergencies. One can't tell for what in advance. Societies always have a treasury. To help unmarried mothers, for instance."

Gisèle burst into a peal of laughter, and I thought the sudden radiance of her grave face the loveliest sight possible.

"I was expecting that!" she cried. "It's a mania of Sara's. Well, I say no, my dear! I won't undertake

never to marry. I consider that even if a woman marries, she can keep her liberty; and besides she doesn't
necessarily keep it in free love, where the children are
no less a burden than in a legal marriage."

This declaration enlightened me a little. Without it
I shouldn't have understood what Sara's mania was;
but I didn't dare ask for explanations for fear of being
considered too ignorant or too silly. It was the first
time I had heard the expression "unmarried mothers"; it had no exact meaning for me, and if it shocked
me a little, I couldn't have said why. I had long can-
didly believed that in order to have children it was
necessary to be married. And yet I knew they were the
natural result of intimate relations between the sexes.
My mother had thought it right to inform me of this
and to tell me that human beings in this respect did
not differ from animals. But I associated these intimate relations so closely with the state of marriage
that I did not think them possible without it. And yet
I knew that sometimes men and women lived together
without being married. The slightest reflection would
have opened my eyes; but I had in fact never reflected
about it. The little theoretical knowledge I had was
totally unconnected with real life.

My brain was paralyzed at the moment by the presence of Gisèle and Sara; I put off going into the matter till later. The only thing that seemed clear was
that Sara did not intend to marry, but neither did she
intend to live alone. I took refuge behind Gisèle.

"Before committing myself," I said to her, "I shall wait for you to decide."

I hoped for an answer, but she turned to Sara.

"Look here, Sara," she said, "it'll be a very good thing to found a league, but let the pledge only be not to do anything against our consciences or for the sake of imitation."

"Or in order to conform to custom," added Sara.

"Ye-e-s," said Gisèle rather hesitatingly. Then, turning to me, "I think we can promise that," she said. "Now, we will clasp our right hands, as they do for the oath of the Rütli in *William Tell,* and say: 'I swear to be faithful to the I.F.' "

This was done with great solemnity.

Then there was a long silence, as there is after taking Communion.

"What are you thinking of?" said Sara suddenly to Gisèle.

"I'm thinking," answered Gisèle, "of what *I.F.* means in English—*if*—and that our pledge is a little conditional."

"Oh, if you're beginning to back out of it already—"

At that moment Sara's mother raised the portiere that separated the room where we were from the studio.

"I've come for you, my dears. Some girls are wanted to help with the refreshments."

I think I have faithfully reported our conversation.

Today it seems to me extremely childish. But at the time it was of the greatest importance for me, and for days I could not help thinking of it.

When it was time to take leave of our hosts, Mamma went up to Gisèle and to my surprise she said:

"I hear that you live near by, but it's on our way home. Shall we take you back?"

I had already spoken to Mamma about Gisèle, and she knew how much this offer would please me. She wanted to talk to Gisèle just as she had wanted to know Sara.

"Your mother lets you go out alone," said Mamma when we were outside. "She has confidence in you and I'm sure you deserve it."

"I want so much to deserve it," said Gisèle, smiling, "that I never dare do anything. I think I should deserve it much less if she were stricter." Gisèle said this so sweetly and with such perfect naturalness and sprightly grace that I was certain my mother must be pleased. I felt it and was delighted.

"But you aren't strict with Geneviève either, madame," she went on. "You don't always take her to school. She often comes by herself." (Had she really noticed this?)

"I go with her whenever I can," said my mother, "not because I don't trust her but because I like being with her. I shall miss her very much if she ever leaves me."

"That's what my mother says too."

Gisèle's tone had become very grave again. I understood that she loved her mother dearly and suddenly reproached myself with not loving mine enough. We walked on for some time without speaking. I didn't know where my new friend lived and was sorry when I heard Mother say suddenly:

"Here we are already at your door, I think. Mademoiselle Gisèle, it would be kind of you to tell your mother I should like very much to know her."

As soon as Gisèle had left us, I squeezed affectionately up to Mamma.

"What's the matter, Geneviève darling? You'll be knocking me down!" said she, putting her arm round me.

"I think I've only just begun this evening to understand how sweet you are."

She pretended to laugh so as to hide her emotion. Then, as if nothing had happened, "Ugh!" she said, "after that smoky studio it's refreshing to walk home."

I have said nothing so far about my brother. Although he was only a year younger than I, he took no great part in my life. As his health was delicate, he had been more petted than I. I don't think it was that that put me against him, but rather a kind of way he had of flattering my father so as to get what he wanted. He always succeeded. My father had never raised his hand against Gustave, whereas I shall never forget that he once gave me a slap. He had just, like Solomon, advised my brother and me to take example from the ant; I was only nine at the time and I had been bold enough to say:

"But, Daddy, you often tell us we mustn't behave like animals."

Oh, it isn't the slap I object to (I have often given my own son corporal punishment), but it was too obvious that Papa slapped me because he could think of no other answer and in order to punish me for noticing his inconsistency. As for Gustave, he wasn't in the least disturbed by inconsistency; he followed my father's example in habitually modifying his talk, his tastes, his thoughts, to suit the moment's requirements. I have said that he flattered my father; he did this by pretending to admire everything that dropped from his mouth; but I think that what he really admired was the ease with which my father changed his opinions as if they were clothes.

This enabled Gustave to quote him on every possible occasion and constantly to take cover behind "as Papa says." He did this all the oftener because he knew it exasperated me. He speedily ceased to apply his mind to anything he did not think useful and profitable—of immediate and practical profit, I mean, to himself. Although we lived under the same roof, we rarely spoke to each other; he shared none of my tastes. I thought it was indifference on his part. I did

not suspect the hostility to me that was slowly growing in the dark. It burst out suddenly soon after the
moment I have reached in my story. A one-man show
of Keller's latest works had just been opened. The
newspapers spoke of it and particularly praised the
most important of the pictures; it was called *L'Indolente* and a reproduction of it came out in *L'Illustration*. It represented a nude young woman lying on a
divan and looking at herself in a hand-mirror that
hid her face.

I had heard Keller declare that for him the subject
of a picture had no importance; the only thing that
mattered was the quality of the painting. Everybody
agreed that in this case it was "magnificent" and I
was glad of it because of Sara. I have said that my
father looked very much askance at my friendship
with her. Gustave found means to curry favor with
him by treacherously working against my friend. He
knew that I frequently saw her out of school hours
and that I was getting more and more attached to
her; moreover, I had been so imprudent as to praise
her in his presence, and this was why he wanted to
disparage her.

The scene took place immediately after lunch,
which had passed off in a silence that foreboded
thunder. It was my father's custom to read the paper
during this meal. He usually interlarded his reading
with remarks upon the political situation, as though
to lessen or excuse his want of courtesy to my mother

in reading. The paper was placed every day beside his plate; but this morning he left it unopened. His frowning brows, his stern looks, showed that he was silent not because he had nothing to say but because he did not want to speak just then—he was saving it up. A storm was brewing, and it was on my head it would break; I was certain of it, for Gustave, who no doubt knew what was coming, kept looking at me with a spiteful grin. We were having coffee in my father's study. I say "we" because Father's coffee was a collective ceremony, but actually he was the only one to drink it.

As we came out of the dining-room, he had dismissed Gustave, who, as I found out afterward, had gone into the next room and applied his ear to the keyhole so as not to lose any of the scene he had so slyly prepared.

My father was well aware that there was nothing he could do with me; foreseeing my resistance, he turned to my mother for help in crushing it, and it was she he addressed, suddenly bursting out and thumping the table at which he was sitting, not with his fist, for that would have been vulgar, but with the flat of his hand.

"I will not tolerate Geneviève's associating with that Keller girl any longer."

This was said in a tone that admitted of no reply; but Mamma in her calmest voice asked:

"Do you intend to remove her from the *lycée*?"

Father did not feel equal to a struggle with the two of us together; I felt Mamma on my side, and that gave me great courage.

"We will remove her if necessary," he said, as if to associate her with himself. "In the meantime I categorically" (this was a favorite word of his) "object to her seeing that little Keller out of school hours. You understand, don't you?" he cried, thumping the table again with the flat of his hand, but so disastrously that his coffee spoon leaped up and hit him on the nose. Like a malicious fairy, the little coffee spoon spoiled his effect. I could hardly suppress a silly laugh. Father knew, for that matter, that I didn't take him seriously. But this put the finishing touch to his fury.

"This is no time for joking," he said.

I bent down hastily to pick up the spoon; then as I raised my head, without looking at him, however, so as to tone down my insolence and not too obviously flout him, "I have no intention," I said, "of obeying you."

There was a painful silence. I could see that Mamma was very pale and that Papa's hands were trembling.

"Geneviève," he said at last, "take care. You will force us to have recourse to—" But not knowing to what he would have recourse, he corrected himself: "—force us to be severe."

Then, turning to my mother, "Read this," he said

with great solemnity. And Papa took from his inside coat pocket a newspaper clipping, or rather a magazine clipping, which he unfolded and held out to her.

"Read it aloud, please."

"Gustave gave you that?" Mamma said without taking the piece of paper. And she added in a lower voice: "Little wretch!"

"That's right!" cried Papa violently; "you're going to blame *him* now."

Then Mamma, still apparently very calm, but so pale that I expected to see her faint, said: "As a matter of fact, I've already read that disgusting article."

"Then why didn't you inform us of it?"

"Because I thought there was no need to pay any attention to it."

"But what is it all about?" I asked, taking up the piece of paper, which had fallen to the floor.

This is what I read under the heading "What People Say":

It was Mademoiselle Sara Keller, the celebrated painter's own daughter, who posed for the magnificent nude that everybody admires at the exhibition. Our congratulations to the painter and his model. The picture is the choicest of morsels and we are grateful to the painter for introducing us in this way to the intimacy of his family life. If some prudish moralists are scandalized, let us repeat to Alfred Keller in the words of Baudelaire:

> Half close old Plato's austere eye
> To paint the secret of this maid in flower.

Art and modesty seldom go hand in hand.

I shrugged my shoulders.

"And is that why you want to stop my seeing Sara?"

Father again turned toward Mamma.

"Is it tolerable, I ask you, that Geneviève should go on being intimate with a shameless girl who doesn't mind exposing herself to the public gaze stark naked?"

"If that disgusting journalist had kept silent," I said, "nobody would have suspected it was she"—an imprudent remark, which put me in the wrong and enabled Father to say:

"Even if nobody had known anything about it, the fact would have been there none the less. It isn't other people's opinions I care about, it's the thing itself, as you know."

I knew exactly the contrary: my father cared a great deal about other people's opinions; indeed, he cared about nothing much else; but I had given myself away.

"So then," he went on, "you knew about it?"

"No, I didn't know. But if I had known, it wouldn't have altered my feelings for Sara. And if I had known, I should have taken good care not to say anything to you about it."

"Geneviève!" said my mother severely.

Papa pretended to be astonished.

"What! Don't you take her part?"

"I have never approved of her insolence."

"Nevertheless, it's always to you she goes for support against me. But that's not the point. . . . Then, Geneviève, you're determined not to obey me?"

"Absolutely determined."

He appeared to hesitate for a little; then, as if making a decision: "Very well. I know now what I must do," he said loftily.

He didn't know in the least, and, as a matter of fact, he did nothing.

When I told my father that even if I had known that Sara had posed in the nude for her father, it wouldn't have altered my feelings for her, I was telling a lie. I realized this as soon as I was alone. With my heart in an indescribable turmoil, I ran to the drawing-room to look for the number of *L'Illustration* in which a reproduction of Keller's picture had appeared. I had not seen the picture itself—only this photograph. Now that I knew that this naked woman was Sara, I wanted to see it again; I hadn't looked at it enough. The number of *L'Illustration* was lying on the table, but when I opened it, I found to my amazement that the reproduction had been removed, carefully cut out—by Gustave, I guessed at once. I rushed to his room. He had obviously just sat down at his table, but he pretended to be plunged in work.

"You might knock before you come in," he said without raising his nose from an atlas.

I struggled to keep calm, but my voice trembled with indignation.

"Did you take that photo out of *L'Illustration?*"

"What photo?" he asked, pretending innocence, and with the most irritating little smile.

"Don't pretend not to understand. You know perfectly well what I mean. Who gave you leave to cut out that photo?"

He gave me a defiant grin.

"Perhaps I ought to have asked your permission?"

"Gustave, you're to give me back that photo at once."

"That photo! That photo! In the first place, that photo isn't yours."

I flung myself upon him in a frenzy. Before he had time to ward me off, I had lifted the atlas; the picture was underneath it; I seized hold of it. But Gustave, who had suddenly collected himself, snatched it from my hands and tore it into little bits.

"That's what she deserves, Miss Sara Keller, your dear friend!"

We stood for a moment, glaring, ready to spring at each other, and panting. Gustave was no stronger than I. In a fight I think I should have got the better of him. But what next? . . . Besides, he didn't give me time for reflection; he darted to the door as though

he had been seized with terror and began shouting:
"Help! Help!"

I heard the door of my father's study open. I had
just time to run to my room, shut myself in, and fling
myself on my bed sobbing. My head was aching violently and I tried not to think. What distressed me
most was that I was not able to rebel sincerely against
my father's judgment, that in spite of myself I felt
scandalized at the thought that Sara could have ex-
hibited herself in this way, shown herself without any
clothes on and to her father. The very title the painter
had given his picture—*L'Indolente*—seemed to point
to Sara by evoking the woman bathing in the *Orientales*, that Sara *"belle d'indolence"* of whom I have
already said my friend reminded me.

I was in the dark now; I had drawn my curtains
and shut my eyes; but visions of the lovely tawny
body danced wildly about me.

I heard a gentle knock at the door, then Mamma's
low voice:

"Geneviève, my darling, let me in."

She took me in her arms, put her hand on my forehead, calmed me like a child. She had come, she said,
fearing that I was unwell. She didn't say a word about
the recent scene, but took care to let me know that my
father had gone out with Gustave. It was a Thursday
afternoon—a half-holiday at the *lycée*.

"It's very fine; we ought to go out too. Do you
know—supposing we went to see the Keller exhibi-

tion? We might walk there; it would do you good."

I kissed her with all my heart, bathed my red eyes, got ready, and then whispered in her ear:

"Sara said that no one was kinder than Madame Parmentier; but that's because she didn't know you."

Just as we were on the point of entering the art dealer's where the Keller exhibition was being held, Mother stopped abruptly.

"All the same," said she, "I should like to be certain we shan't meet the Kellers—or your father."

She sometimes had these little sudden terrors—as if part of herself ceased to approve her native temerity; but they only lasted a moment.

"Oh! well," she said, making up her mind with a kind of playful recklessness, "what does it matter? We shall soon see. In we go!"

Fortunately there was no one we knew in the gallery. And fortunately too a good many landscapes, still-lifes, and portraits dispersed the attention of the visitors, so that they weren't obliged to stand exclusively fixed in front of "the magnificent nude." It was hanging in the place of honor and at once attracted the eye. Mother gazed at it without showing any embarrassment, which was very reassuring.

"Very fine!" I heard her murmur.

I was accustomed to nudities in museums and admired with no thought of ill such celebrated pictures as the *Odalisque*, the *Source*, the *Olympia*, or the *Déjeuner sur l'herbe*. But I could not get out of my mind that the young woman I saw there with no clothes on was Sara, my Sara, and for that reason, no doubt, the picture seemed to me extremely indecent.

I wanted to be alone in the room; the other people's eyes embarrassed me; I felt, whenever I looked at the big canvas, that they were observing me. And yet, in spite of my heart-ache and my embarrassment, I was attracted by the extraordinary beauty of the *"indolente"* and filled with a strange and disturbing feeling such as I had never before experienced.

Someone had quietly stolen up behind me, and all of a sudden I felt two cool hands laid upon my eyes. I turned round. It was Gisèle.

"What fun to meet here!" she cried. Then she caught sight of my mother.

"I gave your message to Mamma and she said she would like to know you very much too. She came with me. Only I'm not at all good at introducing people." Then taking her mother by the arm and leading her up to us: "Mamma," she said awkwardly, "Madame X, my new friend's mother; but of course you don't know Geneviève either. Well, here she is."

Gisèle's mother was charming and I felt at once that Mother liked her. She spoke French very well, but with a strong accent, which was rather attractive and seemed to add to her natural distinction. We were in front of the big picture.

"It must be acknowledged that Monsier Keller is

very talented," said Mother after the exchange of a few polite commonplaces.

"And at any rate he isn't afraid of choosing good-looking models. Painters nowadays seem so often to be afraid of beauty."

I wondered with much anxiety whether Mme Parmentier knew of the scandal. But her tone of voice reassured me. There was nothing in it to allow one to suspect irony or hidden meanings. As for recognizing Sara, it was impossible. Mother too seemed reassured, for she had certainly shared my anxiety.

"And afraid too of painting a picture that really represents something," said she. "Painters nowadays seem to want to puzzle us more than anything else."

I stopped listening to our mothers; while they were going on with a conversation so happily begun, I drew Gisèle a little aside.

What did she know? With a trembling voice and in a great state of agitation I asked: "Did you know that Sara—"

But she didn't let me finish. "I even went to see her sit," said she, as if it was the most natural thing in the world.

This little sentence struck into my heart like a knife. So there existed between my two best friends an intimacy I had no suspicion of. Why did Sara keep me at a distance? Oh, no doubt I should have felt embarrassed at seeing her naked. But it was not for her to consider a modesty that I myself was quite ready to renounce. And as for being embarrassed, I was far more so at the idea that she had shown herself naked to Gisèle. But it wasn't modesty in this case; no, it was jealousy.

"Not a word to Mother! She doesn't suspect anything," added Gisèle. And when I told her that my mother had learned it from a horrid article in the press, "I hope she won't say anything about it," she said.

I quickly reassured her.

On leaving the exhibition Mme Parmentier had the happy thought of inviting us to tea in a neighboring teashop. My mother and she seemed to get on exceedingly well and never stopped talking; but Gisèle and I remained silent. At the moment of saying good-by, I was going to return the catalogue of the exhibition that Mme Parmentier had lent me, but she refused to take it.

"No, Geneviève, keep it in remembrance of this delightful afternoon."

I was glad to keep it because of the very good reproduction of the picture it contained, and as soon as I got home, I shut myself up in my room to gaze at it at my leisure. My imagination strove to clothe that lovely, lithe body in the dress that Sara usually wore at school—that everyday dress I saw her wearing the next morning, of which I found it far easier to imagine her divested. Yes, my eyes, in spite of myself, undressed her and I imagined her as the *Indolente*.

I was racked by unfamiliar pangs, which I did not know to be desire, because I thought desire could only be felt for a person of the opposite sex; and at times, when I saw Sara's hand resting on the desk in front of us, my own hand crept toward it involuntarily—for I had lost all control over myself—and then withdrew abruptly if Sara noticed my movement; and all that Friday morning I stayed without saying a single word to her, without saying anything to Gisèle, either; and when I saw them both going away together after school, my heart was torn with a dreadful unhappiness, for hadn't Mamma said the evening before that I was not to associate with Sara after school hours?

Yes, that Thursday evening, shortly after our return from the exhibition, Mother had come to me in my room.

"Geneviève, my darling child," she had begun in her tenderest voice—a voice that made my heart melt and left me powerless to resist—"I have thought over what I am going to say very carefully; it grieves me very much to be obliged to pain you. . . ."

She hesitated for a moment or two, but I knew already what was coming, and I began murmuring: "I can't. I can't."

She went on: "I don't want you to misunderstand me. It's for your good I'm asking this of you. Your friendship for Sara makes me uneasy. I am afraid it may hold a great deal of suffering in store for you, and that it may lead you farther than you want to go."

She had seated herself and taken me on her knees as she used to do. With my head on her shoulder, I began to sob:

"Oh, Mamma, you don't understand. You can't understand."

But there was no doubt she realized the violence of my passion; and it was that very thing that made her uneasy.

"Geneviève, my darling, I think I understand you only too well, and better perhaps than you understand yourself. That is why I am obliged to warn you. I am afraid you are embarking on a dangerous course, one that will be much more difficult for you to abandon later on."

She certainly did not dare say all she meant and it was for me to understand her thought behind her words. Then, as I could think of no argument, I came out with an absurd sentence, which I immediately regretted:

"But, Mamma, if I stop seeing her, it'll look as if I were obeying Papa."

"Oh, Geneviève," said she, "that ugly thought is unworthy of you! I'm sure you're ashamed of it already."

"And then—and then," I sobbed, "what do you want me to do? You know I see her every day at school; she sits next to me. . . . What do you want me to say to her? . . ."

"I can ask the principal to change your seat."

"Oh, no, Mamma, don't do that, I implore you. At any rate let me see her."

"But it's that that's hurting you, my poor child. Oh, I wish so much I could help you, against yourself. . . ."

What the next morning was like I have already told. I could pay no attention to the lessons. When I came home to lunch, I was in such a state of agitation that Mother was evidently alarmed. As for my father, he had found a way of punishing me; it was to appear not to be aware of my presence. But what better could I wish for? After the meal Mother came to my room, where I had shut myself up.

"Are you ill, my poor Geneviève? You're all trembling, and you didn't eat anything at lunch. . . ."

Sick, my heart was certainly so. I reassured my mother, however, but begged her not to send me back to the *lycée*. To go on seeing Sara and to treat her coldly, when my whole being longed for her, was really beyond my strength. The danger must have seemed very great to my mother, for she consented to keep me at home. My father had an easy triumph. He had always disapproved of the *lycée*. According to him, women didn't need instruction so much as good manners; and he added that all sensible people, including Molière, thought the same. This was by no means my opinion, nor, very fortunately, my mother's. I was very greedy for knowledge. Everything I was taught at school interested me much; and it would be my education, I thought dimly even then, that would later enable me to become independent. I intended to go up for the *baccalauréat* examination the following year and not to draw the line there. It was arranged I should leave the *lycée* for reasons of health. Must I stop seeing Gisèle? My mother had taken a great liking to Mme Parmentier, and to Gisèle too, for that matter. She thought that an explanation of my absence was due to them. The embarrassing thing was that Gisèle was Sara's friend. I spent a few days in a state of great distraction. I had agreed to submit to my mother's decisions. I felt that she was in continual opposition to my father, and my resistance to paternal authority was strengthened by my filial obedience to her. But had not friendship too its duties—even without considering the solemn vow pronounced at the founding of the I.F.? And what would Gisèle and Sara think of me? What self-respect could I keep if I allowed them to think that I had suddenly banished them from my heart? I implored my mother to let me speak to Gisèle, and she promised to go herself to see Mme Parmentier and arrange with her that I should have a private talk with her daughter. I have no idea what Mother said to Mme Parmentier, but when she came back from her call her face was sparkling and she had a dimple in each cheek.

"Do you know what Madame Parmentier suggested?" she said at once. "That she should give you an English lesson every day. She proposes you should go to her during the time Gisèle is at the *lycée,* for she thinks, as I do, that you and Gisèle had better not meet too often on account of Sara."

"Then you spoke to her about Sara? You told her—?"

"There was nothing to tell her, dear Geneviève. Gisèle herself had told her mother everything the day after we met at the exhibition."

"And yet she begged me not to say anything about it."

"Well, you see, her confidence in her mother carried the day," said Mamma. Then she added, rather ingenuously: "It's true Madame Parmentier had just come across that horrid article."

"But Madame Parmentier hasn't forbidden Gisèle to see Sara."

"No. That shows we think a little differently about the matter. And then she knows Gisèle is more sensible than you are."

"Or that she doesn't love Sara as much as I do."

"Less passionately than you do; yes, no doubt."

If I have dwelt at such length on this early passion of my youth it is on account of the first vague stirring of my senses. Immediately after the events I have related, I fell ill. Scarlet fever, in which, as Freud would say, the profound disturbance of my whole being took refuge, came to the rescue of my mother and myself. My mother told me afterward that during the first few days of delirium (for I had a very high temperature) I was haunted by Sara's image. But when I began to recover, my ideas had taken another direction.

PART

ii

MME PARMENTIER was a good deal better educated than my mother, who had not begun to read methodically and carefully till rather late in life. The lessons she gave me were quite different from those I had attended at the *lycée* and consisted chiefly of conversation and reading. In the big library where she received me, English authors neighbored with French and Italian ones, for she spoke the three languages equally well. My mother came with me to begin with, but left us after the third lesson, when Mme Parmentier confessed she would be more at her ease if she had me to herself. Usually she made me read aloud and devoted herself to correcting my bad accent. I liked it better when it was she who read to me, though often enough I didn't understand very well; but then she would begin again with infinite patience. The sound of her voice enchanted me almost as much as Sara's. Poets were her favorites, and it was her theory that they would be particularly helpful in teaching me to accentuate my sentences properly. But I couldn't long conceal from her how little I cared for dreams and poetry. Then we began to argue.

"Flowers, it is true," she said, "don't nourish

mankind, but they are the joy of life. If you turn all the loveliest and sweetest-smelling flower-beds into kitchen gardens, you will no doubt provide me with enough to eat, but at the same time you will deprive me of any wish to live."

And as I replied that my mind could no more live on comparisons than my body on flowers, she smiled mournfully and exclaimed: "Oh, if now you've taken a dislike even to images!"

In this way she took pleasure in an imaginary world, which, she declared, existed as soon as she began to believe in it. She believed too in the life everlasting, and the compensations she expected here-after helped her to bear with resignation the ills and imperfections of this earth.

Even at that time I was less attached to fiction than to reality, and novels interested me not so much for the beauty of their descriptions as for the information they gave me about life. This explains why in writing this account I only concern myself with what may possibly be—however slightly—of some information or instruction. I don't myself care enough for amusement to attempt to amuse others. What I wish, rather, is to *warn* them. I think, M. Gide, that you yourself have used this word as I do here. Allow me to borrow it from you. Yes, I shall be satisfied if some young woman reading this finds in it a *warning* and if this book puts her on her guard against a number of illusions that caused me great suffering and came near to wrecking my life.

"A stranger to the subtleties of thought, and caring nothing for metaphysics." I read these words yesterday in Marthe de Fels's fine study of Vauban. They describe me exactly. In the same book I read another sentence that delighted me and in which I recognize myself: "The realism of his concrete mind, in which the cloudy vapor of dreams was never allowed sanctuary when the moment called for action. . . ." For young as I was at that time, I resolutely believed that I might be and ought to be useful. Poetry—literature even—seemed to me the flowers of an idle life; and I had a horror of idleness.

I have been led on to define certain traits of my character of which I only became conscious later on as they grew more marked. My opposition to Mme Parmentier, in spite of the great affection I had for her, was a great help to me. We develop in an atmosphere of sympathy, but we only come to know ourselves in opposition. This opposition, however, had nothing in common with the feeling that animated me against my father, which was aggravated by contempt. For Mme Parmentier I had nothing but esteem. In spite of our disagreements, we got on admirably together, and she was touched by the zeal with which I worked. Nevertheless I needed other lessons than hers, and my mother had recourse to a professor to teach me history and geography. Dr. Marchant, overworked as he was, agreed to give me an hour every other day for science. These lessons took place in his house in the evenings and were often prolonged in talks, which were more profitable to me than the lessons themselves.

Dr. Marchant had all that my father lacked; in the first place, sterling worth, sound knowledge, and a complete contempt for all shams and pretenses. His grumpy manners hid a tender heart. The admiration I felt for him did not prevent me from being in opposition to him too, but for still other reasons. As our lessons and conversations did not come to an end even after I had passed my examinations, but continued more actively than before, it is possible that what I am about to say may relate to 1914 or even a little later and that it was only when my judgment was rather more formed that I became aware of certain traits of his character with which I could not sympathize. His devotion, his absolute disinterestedness, that kind of ardent charity which makes him so tender to suffering, were all based on hopeless nihilism. As for me, who never had very lively feelings about religion (and those which my father professed were enough to disgust me with it), I very soon ceased to believe in any sort of unreality. But whereas Dr. Marchant accepted the rooted misery of mankind, "which at best," he said, "we can only slightly alleviate," I could not admit that our hopes need stop at that. He treated me as utopian when I spoke of a possible improvement in the social conditions of man-

kind, and this drove me wild; I spoke no doubt as a
child and my words evidently laid me open to ridi-
cule. I felt it, but I clung to my utopia. I clung hard.
This hope which is still mine has guided my life. At
that time it was very vague and I should have done
better perhaps to wait before speaking of it. I did so
out of impatience.

I have reread what I have just written and am not
at all satisfied with it. When one ceases to be a member of a church, how hazardous, uncertain, and over-
bold seems any profession of faith! I have recently
read in an American review the answers to a question-
naire entitled "What do you believe?" It was addressed to the most famous writers, scholars, states-
men, financiers, industrialists, etc., of all countries.
The only ones who seemed to answer with any assurance were those who belonged to the Catholic Church.
But the real answer of the others is their entire work,
their life. It is possible to hesitate when it is a question
of words and be decided when it comes to deeds.
Theories are no affair of mine and I know very well
what I want, though I am very bad at saying it. For
that matter, if I had been able to express it in a few
words, I should not have embarked upon this long
story.

Mme Marchant had been a childhool friend of
my mother's. Modest to excess, almost insignificant
—at any rate, this is what I thought her at that time
of my life, for at that age I was little inclined to look

for what lies beneath the surface and despised modesty. If my father stood in my eyes for the type of man I would not marry for anything in the world, Mme Marchant stood for the type of woman I was determined not to be. Nothing, in my eyes, justified the love the doctor showed her; she seemed negligible to me. She lived in the shadow of her devotion to her husband. They were certainly a most united couple, in spite of the doctor's cynical remarks about marriage, which he considered "a ridiculous institution." He had no scruple in pronouncing these words before me, young as I was at the time, and in spite of the furious glances of my father, who professed the greatest respect for "that sacred institution."

Instructed early by my mother, who held that ignorance could never be of the slightest benefit to anyone, I knew that children were not the spontaneous result of the marriage sacrament; I understood too that the physical relationship that permits the procreation of children often dispenses with the approval of the Church and the laws. But once people were married, why did some couples remain childless? This puzzled me greatly, especially when I thought of our friends the Marchants.

"That is a frightfully indiscreet question," said my mother when I put it to her. "But you know I hardly ever refuse to answer you. . . . In the first place, a great many married couples prefer not to have children."

"Why?"

"For numbers of more or less sound reasons, moral or material."

"How do they manage not to have any?"

"Really, my dear, that's not a thing you need know for the present," said Mamma, blushing a little, no doubt less at my question than at her own reluctance to answer it.

And yet I had put the question quite innocently and without any suspicion of its indecency. Having so far only the vaguest ideas about sexual desire and pleasure, the question of conjugal intercourse interested me far less than that of offspring.

"Do you think the Marchants prefer not to have children?" I asked.

"No, I don't think so," said Mother, and then added very quickly: "But one doesn't always get what one wants."

"Then do you think they'd like to have children but can't?"

"You see, darling, how dangerous it is to start answering your questions," said Mother, her hand on the doorknob and beating a retreat. "You always want to know more and more."

The fact is that these few sentences of my mother's left me extremely unsatisfied. And as the question remained unsolved in my mind, I determined, with the ruthless and naïve intrepidity of my youthful years, to put it to the doctor directly; but for that I

had to get a moment alone with him, and Mme Marchant was nearly always present at my lessons. This
conversation, therefore, didn't take place till after
the holidays.

These, which I spent in Brittany with some cousins,
I occupied almost entirely in reading.

Questions of a sexual order, on which it may surprise or shock some people to see me dwell in this
narrative, were likewise those that chiefly interested
me in the books I read. My curiosity, however, was
unmixed with any sensuality. It had needed all the
prestige of Sara's voice to make me take pleasure in
Baudelaire's poetry. A sort of instinctive fear kept
me away from licentious pictures, from all that
breathes desire or pleasure. I was not sentimental
either. No, my mind was occupied with everything
that touched upon what are pompously called
women's rights. I have said that I was not interested in novels. The sorrows of love did not seem
to me worth the trouble of describing. But a book
sometimes found grace in my eyes for the sake of a
single sentence, like the one I found in that absurd
Jane Eyre and copied out then and there in the notebook I kept for this purpose, on which were inscribed
as title the two letters I.F. in memory of the league
for Indépendance Féminine and of my two first
friends.

"It is vain to say human beings ought to be satisfied with tranquillity: they must have action; and

they will make it if they cannot find it. Millions are condemned to a stiller doom than mine, and millions are in silent revolt against their lot. Nobody knows how many rebellions besides political rebellions ferment in the masses of life which people earth. Women are supposed to be very calm generally: but women feel just as men feel; they need exercise for their faculties, and a field for their efforts as much as their brothers do; they suffer from too rigid a restraint, too absolute a stagnation, precisely as men would suffer; and it is narrow-minded in their more privileged fellow-creatures to say that they ought to confine themselves to making puddings and knitting stockings, to playing on the piano and embroidering bags. It is thoughtless to condemn them, or laugh at them, if they seek to do more or learn more than custom has pronounced necessary for their sex." (*Jane Eyre*, Ch. xii.)

Of all the books I read at that time, none occupied my thoughts longer than *Clarissa Harlowe*. Notwithstanding my small liking for fiction, it was without skipping a line that I read the seven volumes of that novel which was once so celebrated and which nowadays, I believe, does not find many readers. There is no doubt it had a considerable influence on me (though not, I think, of the kind that Richardson himself would have desired); and for that reason I must speak of it. I first of all remarked that all

Clarissa's misfortunes come from her devotion and
submission to her parents, her respect for her odious
father. It needed all Richardson's art, I thought, not
to make this excessive humility appear ridiculous in
our eyes. By endowing her with all the virtues, by
making her infinitely superior to her father, the
novelist renders this angel's submission to the monstrous authority of such a narrow-minded, hide-
bound creature all the more revolting.

But what made me still more indignant was the supreme importance this book attributes to chastity.
Although Clarissa's virtue never shows more trium-
phantly than after she has been treacherously vio-
lated, this assimilation of honor with purity seemed
to me absolutely inadmissible. In those days I could
not know how often the soul itself is disintegrated by
the act of physical yielding. For that matter, a great
deal of willful prejudice entered into my indignation
at that time, and my sincerest reactions were soon to
teach me how different I was from the person I set up
to be. Be that as it may, I maintained that a good
woman is not to be judged merely by her modesty,
and that her greater or less degree of virtue resides
elsewhere than on the plane of sexual relations. All
this still bore the mark of the conversations I had had
with my two friends, in which we had defiantly pushed
to extremes our scorn of convention and public opinion. Our talk was all the bolder because it was un-
accompanied by the participation of our senses. We

all three allowed that physical ties might dispense
with legal authority; we were all three cheerfully resolved upon motherhood outside of marriage; but if
I, for my part, spoke so easily and lightly of love, it
was because I thought only of its results, without any
notion, or even apprehension of physical pleasure, so
that I imagined I should always be able to dispose
of myself with perfect freedom. Certainly my agitation in Sara's proximity might have forewarned me,
but though it shook me to my depths, it was in too
vague a manner for me to recognize it as desire. Without the help of some early initiation, desire may remain unlocalized and only show itself at first by general upheaval. After all, what I am saying was perhaps only true of myself. Sara, I think, was much less
innocent, and a secret lasciviousness added no doubt
to the attraction of her beauty; it was that, I think,
which upset me so.

I had known Dr. Marchant from my earliest childhood, and for a long time I could not understand why
my mother had not married him rather than my
father. But from a conversation I once had with
Mother, and later on from her journal, I learned that
Dr. Marchant had been introduced to her by my
father and that she had begun by taking a dislike to
him. Evidently at first sight he may seem cold; but
I think it is because he feels he must be on his guard
against his impulsive heart. As soon as he lets himself
go, his eyes brim over with tenderness. I used to hear

him called "materialist" by my father and "pessimist" by my mother long before I knew what those words meant. Later on, when I began to argue with him, it was only against his pessimism that I protested.

"I don't blame you, my child" (he used often to call me "my child," just as my mother did), "for having such ideas." (This he would say when I declared that it would be better to prevent poverty than relieve it.) "They belong to your age. One dreams then of social reforms, of more equitable distribution. But the best systems won't improve men's nature." And he quoted Chamfort's maxim: "The man who is not a misanthrope at the age of forty has never loved men," adding that he was decidedly more than forty.

At that moment, by an unusual chance, the doctor and I were alone.

"How many people we take an interest in," he said too, "simply because they are suffering and wretched! But if they were well and wealthy we should immediately think them repulsive. Heavens! If she isn't crying!"

At that time I used to cry for the slightest thing in spite of my stringent resolve not to, and it made me furious with myself. On that occasion too I had been unable to check my tears; but it was with indignation that I was crying, with vexation at finding nothing to reply, or rather at not being able to express the thoughts that bubbled up in me and sprang not so

much from my brain, I thought, as from my heart. I
was not too young to suspect that many of the ills
from which men suffered were due not so much to real
causes, which in themselves would be very bearable,
as to the judgments pronounced upon them by others.
I had just been reading *Adam Bede* with Mme Parmentier and I was thinking in particular of Hetty
Sorrel's disaster. I would not consent to consider her
guilty for having been seduced and then for abandoning her child in despair, knowing as she did the crushing condemnation that awaited her. What I thought
worthy of condemnation was, in the first place, the
lover who deserted her, and in the next, society, which
visited on her alone the reprobation that was more
justly deserved by her seducer. I wanted to quote her
as an example, but I was afraid Dr. Marchant
wouldn't know the book, and it was with Mme Parmentier that I started the discussion again.

"Would you have condemned Hetty Sorrel?"

"I have no right to condemn anyone."

"That's no answer. I was speaking of a particular
instance and you take refuge in generalities."

"I think I should have taken pity on her as Dinah
Morris did, while recognizing her guilt."

"Guilty of what?"

"What a question! Guilty first of being seduced and
and then of abandoning her child."

"She only abandoned it reluctantly and because she
couldn't do otherwise. It was society's judgment that

forced her to commit the crime. She knew there would be no place in society henceforth for her or for the child. That's what I consider monstrous."

"I take pity on her because she repented."

"And she repented because Dinah Morris got her to believe that her repentance would be followed by God's forgiveness. But the true criminal is not Hetty; it's society. And when one thinks that it's in the name of God that society condemns her! . . ."

"Come, Geneviève, you can't say you approve of her."

"I pity her with all my heart, but it's society I disapprove of. . . . Madame Parmentier, I want to ask you—do you think it's very wicked to have a child without being married?"

"It's very wicked to bring a child into the world which is doomed to be unhappy."

"Why doomed?"

"How can a fatherless child not be unhappy?"

"Oh, Madame Parmentier, you shouldn't say that to *me*. You wouldn't speak so if you knew my father. And besides must a father really be a husband in order to love his child?"

Mme Parmentier went on without answering me:

"A wretched child who runs the risk of never being welcomed anywhere, of being repulsed and insulted everywhere."

"That's what makes me indignant. Don't you think it's monstrous that—"

But she went on without listening:

"Feeling his mother despised and, what's worse, being obliged to despise her himself."

"Oh, Madame Parmentier! How can you say that? Then, according to you, in order to have the right to have children, a woman must consent to be tied during her whole existence to a man whom perhaps she can no longer love?"

"She has only to make a better choice."

"As if it were even she who chooses! You know quite well that more often than not she has to wait to be chosen."

"She is free to refuse if she dislikes the man who proposes to her."

"She may have illusions at first, as I think my mother had."

"Geneviève, you oughtn't to talk so of your parents. I don't know your father well, but he seems to me charming."

"My mother thought him charming when she married him."

"I consider your mother an admirable wife."

"That is to say she has always sacrificed herself. Do you think it's a good thing that a person like my mother should always sacrifice herself to somebody who isn't worth her?"

"A united couple has always to make a few little reciprocal sacrifices; they improve and ennoble those who make them."

"Madame Parmentier—why is simply being unfaithful to one's husband called deceiving him? One
can very well be unfaithful without any deception.
And doesn't one deceive him a great deal more, and
oneself too, by remaining faithful after one has ceased
to love him?"

"Certainly not. What questions you're putting to
me! People may not love each other as much as they
did when they first married, but to love another man
—that's where deceiving begins. As for me, I never
had any merit in being faithful because I never ceased
loving my husband. But even if love becomes a little
less, when one marries one makes a promise to remain
faithful to what one has sworn."

"Yes, so I prefer not to swear."

No doubt I have greatly simplified this conversation, which was a long one. It took place in the spring
of 1914. I remember a huge bunch of lilacs on the big
table in the library, where we were sitting; it had
such a strong scent that Mme Parmentier asked me
to open the window, though the air outside was still
chilly. I ought perhaps to have described the surroundings, and Mme Parmentier, and myself; but I
am not writing a novel and I don't care for descriptions—in other people's books either.

It was in November that I passed the second part
of my *baccalauréat,* for I had stupidly failed in July.
My father's delight at hearing of my failure pricked
my vanity and I worked doubly hard. Gisèle, who

was going in for the same examinations, passed hers
the first time. I used to see her every now and then,
but Mme Parmentier did not encourage our meeting. The freedom of my remarks might amuse *her*,
but they somewhat alarmed her for her daughter. And
yet Gisèle was not easily influenced either by me or
by her mother, whom, however, she adored; but she
was able to hold her own if she wanted to, without
even raising her voice, and with such obstinacy and
disarming gentleness that Mme Parmentier always
ended by giving in.

Gisèle and I thought alike on many subjects, and
it was the most advanced ideas that we especially held
in common. This gave me considerable confidence,
for I trusted greatly to her common sense, which I
thought much superior to mine and incapable of the
exaggerations by which I was often carried away.
Gisèle brought to everything she undertook singular
level-headedness; her intelligence easily dominated
and bridled the impulses of her heart. I never saw her
concede anything to vanity; and for the very reason
that her beauty and wit would have assured her the
greatest success in society, she refused to go into it
and went resolutely on with her studies. It was phi-
lology that attracted her, "if only in memory of my
father," she said to me, "for I think I'm very like
him."

I too, like Gisèle, was determined to go on with my
education and refused to entertain the idea of living

in idleness. More and more were we resolved to make ourselves independent and not be obliged to count on the support of parents or husband—"or lover," we added. For the dishonor, according to us, lay not in having a lover, but in "being kept."

"There are a certain number of careers opening out to women now," I said to Gisèle, "in which I think I might succeed. But they are professions in which the most a woman can do is to make people forget she isn't a man. What I want is— Well, I want a situation that can be filled only by a woman. I am convinced that women are capable of much more and of many other things than is generally supposed and than they themselves know. Up to the present they have never been allowed the possibility of showing their worth. I should like, you see, to invent a career in which I could help women by teaching them to know themselves, to become conscious of their own worth."

"But how? By what means?"

"I don't know yet. At any rate, you're not laughing at me. You don't think what I'm saying too absurd?"

"Not absurd at all. But I think the greater number of women are perfectly satisfied with the subservient condition in which they are kept by the flattery and gallantry of men. The first thing to be obtained is that they themselves should want to change."

"Don't you think that this homage men pay to 'the fair sex' is degrading?"

"Yes, degrading to men."

"And that a woman may aspire to better things than just arousing desires, getting adored, enslaving a man or men?"

"Not to mention that such adoration must be terribly hampering. If I didn't think as you do, I shouldn't go on studying."

"Look here, Gisèle, I firmly believe that there are a great many capable women; that there are a great many more qualities in women than people think, and that these valuable qualities are wasted because nobody knows they exist, because they themselves don't know it, because so far they have never been called upon to show themselves, to come into being."

"Yes, but I believe that a great many valuable qualities, a great deal of virtue, may lie in submission too."

"But submission is just what I object to. In submission these valuable qualities are hidden under a bushel. Women's qualities may be different from men's without being inferior. Why should they be subjected to them?"

"If women weren't beautiful and conscious of being desired, they would have higher ambitions than merely to please."

"How I admire you, Gisèle, for not being satisfied with being beautiful!"

"I don't know about being beautiful; what I care for are the qualities and defects of my mind. Yet I admit I should hate to be ugly, and I should have less heart for my work if it was merely a compensation for me."

"It's not only more education I want for women, but more initiative, more courage, more decision."

"The laws allow us very little."

"Talking of that, I want to go in for the law. It would be a fine thing, don't you think, to study the law from the point of view of one's rights? If it only meant a little more than just passing one's examinations! Women's rights—I should like to learn exactly what they are, not only in France, but in other countries too, so as to be able to give great numbers of women a better idea of what their powers really are."

"And their duties too, I suppose."

"Of course. The greater the power, the greater the duty; yes, I know. But how splendid it would be to take up *new* duties, and to give other women the wish to take them up. I think there are a great many possibilities and needs in us of which we are unaware, which are dormant and which only want a call to arouse them. I should like to say to every woman what for some time past I have been saying every morning to myself: IT LIES WITH YOU."

"To do what?"

"Oh, anything. I think of the story in the Gospels when Christ says to the paralytic: 'Arise and take up thy bed, and walk.' And the woman gets up at once and begins to walk."

"Unfortunately, Geneviève, you aren't Christ, to perform miracles; you won't make the paralyzed walk."

"I don't and don't *want* to believe in miracles. If the woman gets up, it means she was able to. She was able to but she didn't know she was able to. The injunction was necessary, and it was sufficient to make her realize her powers. How far woman's powers go, that is what I should like to get to know well enough not to ask her, not to demand from her anything I'm not certain she's capable of. And, of course, I want to test the strength and virtue of these demands on myself first of all."

Gisèle then drew me to her and kissed me on the forehead.

"I can only repeat," she said, "Christ's words that you quoted: 'Arise and walk.' It lies with you."

It was not till some months later that I was able to have the important conversation with Dr. Marchant that I had long looked forward to. Regular lessons and talks had been continued after my examination. Mme Marchant was always present at them; but she had just been called away to Bayonne to visit an aged relative, and the doctor was waiting for his short holidays to begin in order to join her there. It was therefore some time in July.

I am afraid that my share of the conversation I am about to relate will seem very daring for a young girl

of seventeen; but I repeat that everything I thought
and said at that time was pure theory. It was my mind
alone that pushed forward, and the more audaciously
because it was not in the least concerned by the aloof-
ness of my senses. The cynicism I affected was not
natural; I forced myself to adopt it, and it was not
without a struggle that I spoke as I did. I felt proud
of the victory I gained over myself in thus overcom-
ing my reserve, my timidity, and my modesty. But
now the whole thing seems to me like a kind of stage-
play of which I myself furnished the setting, the problem, and the applauding spectator. One night, then,
I found myself alone with Dr. Marchant in his con-
sulting-room, where he usually received me, and
where I had arrived at half past eight with the firm
intention of speaking to him. I waited for a favorable
moment; but the time was passing. Then, like Julien
Sorel, I gave myself a limit. "If," I said to myself,
"the minute hand goes beyond five minutes past nine
without my having started to say what I have on my
mind, I shall know I am a coward and that henceforth
I shall never be able to count on myself."

The doctor, I remember, was just then talking
about heredity, explaining Mendel's law and telling
me which characteristics were transmissible and
which not. I waited till he stopped for breath, which
he did at four minutes past nine. Then, very quickly,
before he should have time to start off again, with
eyes shut and clenched fists, feeling as I did when I

dived off the high diving-board before I was a very good swimmer, I took the plunge, my heart beating so violently that I was afraid I shouldn't be able to get to the end of my sentence.

"Uncle Marchant" (this is what I used to call him), "I want to know whether you didn't want to have any children or whether you couldn't have them."

He gave a laugh—rather a forced one, I thought.

"Well! Talking of sudden mutations!" said he, in allusion to what he had just been telling me, and then, as nothing more followed, I went on:

"You prefer not to answer me, I see. Or perhaps you're afraid to?"

He suddenly became very grave.

"I may as well admit, my dear, that the grief of having no children has been, for both your aunt and me, the one cloud in our married life. The only cloud," he went on rather solemnly, "but it's a big one. The years pass; we both see other people's children getting born and growing up and we can't console ourselves for having none. You see I'm not afraid to speak to you frankly. As for the reasons for this—" After a little hesitation, as if he were looking for the right word, he found "sterility," which he used as though reluctantly and with a slight look of constraint on his face, "—you will allow me, I suppose, not to mention them. And really it's no concern of yours to know anything about it."

"What it concerns me to know," I answered, "is

that it isn't enough to want children in order to have them."

But the most difficult remained to be said; I thought for a moment that my heart would fail me; then I screwed up my courage.

"Uncle Marchant, I must tell you—I want to have a child."

"You're a little young to get married," he said, smiling once more. "But soon, pretty as you are, and with your father's connections" (this was said with a touch of irony, as always when he spoke of my father), "there will be plenty of suitors, and you will only have to choose among them."

"Perhaps—but I don't want to marry."

"Ho! ho!" he said almost sarcastically, and lighting a cigarette to appear more at his ease, for the conversation was obviously taking a turn that embarrassed him. "That's anarchy! After all," he went on when he had taken a few puffs, "it doesn't surprise me much from you."

Then, as he said nothing more, "Do you think it's very wrong?" I asked.

He waited a moment.

"To tell the truth—no. I think it's very imprudent, which isn't the same thing. No doubt, you haven't realized yet the huge difficulties that would make it almost—"

I didn't let him finish. "There are no difficulties that count," I said as calmly as I could, "when one's as determined as I am."

"Look here, my dear," he said in quite a different tone of voice and as though he wanted to cut the conversation short, "you're only a child as yet. We'll talk about it again in a few years, if you haven't changed your mind."

He got up, thinking, I suppose, that this talk had lasted long enough and that it was time for me to go. But I remained seated. He began then pacing up and down the room and suddenly stopped in front of me.

"But may one inquire why you refuse to marry? After all, it's so very much simpler."

It was simpler too not to answer. I couldn't give all my reasons; it would have led to an argument. I was silent. He took a few more paces toward the other end of the room and then came back to me.

"In the first place, it takes two to make a child; you know that."

"I know it."

"Do you love anyone?"

"I know too that love isn't absolutely necessary for such a thing."

"Are you thinking of anyone in particular?"

He was again standing in front of me and looking down at me. I raised my eyes to his and with a great effort whispered:

"Yes—you."

He went off into a great peal of laughter, which sounded to me very unspontaneous.

"Well, I never!" he exclaimed. Then, striding up and down the room, he shrugged his shoulders and repeated twice over: "Well, I never!" Then, turning toward me, "Since when," he asked, "have you got this absurdity into your head?"

I remained quite calm and asked simply:
"Absurdity? Why?"

"Why? Why?" he repeated loudly. Then in a lower voice, but distinctly and sharply: "Because I love my wife," he said. "Now that's enough. Do you hear?" And he left the room without saying good-by.

My heart was beating and my face burning, and I suddenly felt a violent headache. I didn't go away at once, however, and a good thing too, for after a few minutes Uncle Marchant returned. He came up to me and put his hand kindly on my shoulder. When I looked at him, I saw he had been bathing his face.

"Come, my dear," he said in a voice that was almost tender, "you ought really to understand that I wouldn't give your aunt such pain. What! have a child that wouldn't be hers, when it has been such a grief to her not to have been able to give me one? Why, it would break her heart."

His hand was stroking my shoulder; but now my head was lowered. I got up.

"Come," said he, "let's part good friends all the same. But—no, this evening, you don't deserve a kiss."

I pressed the hand he held out to me; and suddenly,

irresistibly, I put my lips to it. Then I fled.

To tell the truth, it was only from that moment that I fell in love with Dr. Marchant, or rather that I imagined I was in love with him. I think I should have incontinently detested him on the contrary if he had encouraged my advances. In any case, my embarrassment would have been extreme and I should have had to make the most violent effort to master it, for my body in no way approved this impetuous excursion of my mind. In like manner my mind was irritated by my body's reserve and determined to disregard it; and I was furious with myself for feeling so shamefaced and modest, in spite of myself. What a child I still was! Ingenuously convinced that it was possible to dispose of body and heart at one's own will, I had the utmost scorn for people who fell in love involuntarily, and was proudly determined never to love anyone I was not resolved to love. I might as vainly and absurdly have resolved not to let my breasts swell. Life had everything still to teach me, and chiefly this—that freedom from love is necessary in order to dispose of oneself in freedom.

I saw Dr. Marchant again not long after. Mme Marchant had returned from Bayonne, but at the end of a few minutes she left the room, contrary to her custom, which made me suppose that the doctor had asked her to leave us alone.

"Listen, my dear," he said at once, "I should be sorry if our conversation the other evening were to leave the smallest embarrassment between us. But that can only be if you agree that I am not to take what you said seriously."

He was sitting at his table and spoke without looking at me. The light from the lamp fell on his handsome features; I looked at his face, his hands, his whole person, and wondered whether I wanted to kiss him, to press him to my heart, to be folded in his embrace. I was obliged, in spite of myself, to answer no. He took up an ivory paper-cutter from the table and passed it over his lips, and decidedly I had no wish to be in the paper-cutter's place. Never mind! I decided nevertheless that I was in love with the doctor. He went on:

"Not perhaps everything you said, but the last thing—useless for me to be more precise. As for the rest—listen, my dear child. It has often happened to me in the course of my career to come across unfortunate girls who had become pregnant out of weakness, carelessness, or love; some of them deliberately, and then generally in the vain hope of keeping a lover. Nearly all of them a great deal more to be pitied than you seem to suspect. But never till now have I come across a woman—a young woman—who thought of having a child without thinking first of love. A child is the consequence, wished for or not, and not inevitable, of something that ought to count first of all much more than the child—of something that you seem not to take into account at all. In order not to consider such a thing monstrous" (and as I ventured to make a gesture, he repeated: "Yes, monstrous!"), "I am obliged to say to myself that you are still a great deal too young to—"

I interrupted him: "Not too young to have a child, I suppose?"

"No, unfortunately!" (I should have said: "alas!") "But to speak of having one."

The doctor had risen and taken a few paces about the room. There was a long silence, which I took care not to interrupt.

"And yet I should like to know what it is that attracts you," he went on at last in an ironical and aggressive voice, taking up his stand in front of me. "Is it pregnancy? Is it the confinement? I can assure you they are neither of them particularly delightful."

I still kept silent, but at each one of his questions I shook my head. He went on:

"Is it the child itself? Nursing it? Changing its diapers? Playing dolls?"

I thought the doctor's questions absurd. He, so sensible as a rule, seemed to be losing his head. In reality, I had never analyzed the constituents of my resolution, but in my particular case I think a great amount—a predominant amount—of protest entered into it. Yes, protest against an established order that I refused to recognize, against what my father called "morals," and more especially still against my father himself, who in my eyes was the symbol of this "morality"; a desire to humiliate him, to mortify him, to make him blush for me, to disown me; a desire too to assert my independence, my revolt, by an act that only a woman could commit, for which I was resolved to take the sole responsibility, without thinking over-much of the consequences. I tried, very haltingly, to explain a little of all this to Marchant. But my fine arguments, which appeared to me conclusive when I kept them to myself, seemed, as I brought them out, more and more deplorably childish. They deserved nothing more, no doubt, than a shrug of the shoulders. I was almost surprised by the kindness of his voice when Marchant said:

"Do you realize, my dear, what it means for a woman who wants her independence to have charge of a child? The thralldom, the slavery of it!"

And as I did not answer, "Decidedly, obstinate as a mule," he said, shrugging his shoulders.

"I own," I said after a longish silence, "I had hoped for something more from you than a reprimand."

"Hoped for what? A piece of advice? Well, I'll give you a very decided one—think about something else."

At that moment we heard my aunt approaching. No doubt she wanted to warn us, for she made more noise than was necessary and even asked in a very loud voice for someone to open the door, as her hands were full. Was she afraid of surprising us? I there and then put a different construction on her continual presence in the room during the doctor's lessons.

She brought in a tray with glasses and orangeade, which we all drank almost in silence, or keeping merely to the rut of insignificant commonplaces, in which I thought she was stuck, because when she was there I stuck in it myself.

As I have said, I only saw Gisèle now at rare intervals, but I was always extremely anxious to hear her opinions. I spoke to her again about my resolve.

"No," she said, "I don't exactly disapprove of it, but we are decidedly very different. I have examined myself carefully—your example, no doubt—and I think, you know, that I am one of the women who are capable of loving only once in a lifetime. And then I ask myself why I shouldn't marry the man I love."

"As for me," I answered, "I couldn't consent to give myself wholly to one man. I rebel against the idea of having to submit my life for good to the man who gives me a child, and I want him on his side too to remain free. Don't you agree that instead of giving onself to one another, one may just lend oneself?"

"But how could you have any esteem for a man who only lent himself to a transaction of that kind, which is of such extreme importance to the woman?"

And as I made no reply, she went on:

"You see, Geneviève, in my opinion, life will end by upsetting all those fine theories of yours. And," she added with a smile, "it'll be so much the better."

Then she began softly humming:

"Nous tromper dans nos entreprises
C'est à quoi nous sommes sujets.
Le matin, je fais des projets
Et le long du jour des sottises." *

"Are those charming lines yours?"

"What an idea!" she answered laughing. "They're by Voltaire. I often repeat them to myself, and I think they might very well do for you too. One day, my poor Geneviève, you'll get carried away just like anybody else, in spite of your fine resolutions; or, what's worse, you'll think you've discovered someone of extraordinary intelligence and a whole heap of virtues, which will exist only in your imagination. And yet you already know well enough what it is to fall in love and that then one has no control over oneself at all."

"What do you mean?"

"I think there's no danger for either of us now in talking of it. You didn't realize, did you, that I was mad about Sara too? Yes, in spite of my grand reputation for good sense, I was completely beside myself; all my good sense consisted in showing it less than you; but it used to keep me awake at nights. Oh, don't be alarmed; nothing ever happened between us; but if she had taken me in her arms, I should have melted like sugar. Fortunately, Sara never suspected it. I

---

* In all we undertake
We constantly go wrong.
My plans are perfect when I wake,
My actions foolish all day long.

only mention it now—quite calmly, as you see—because I want to ask you whether, supposing Sara had been a man, you would have allowed her to give you a child."

Gisèle's confidence had given me a shock. It took a little time before I felt able to answer, but I did so at last with decision:

"No."

"Why not?" asked Gisèle, and added immediately: "It's understood, of course, that I'm putting on one side all consideration of other people's opinions, of maidenly reserve, of conventional morality; but the more one frees oneself from all that, the more important it is to be severe with oneself. You think so, don't you?"

"Certainly; and if I show a hardened front, it is not, as you know, in order to grant myself indulgences."

"Answer, then: no child in Sara's image—why not?"

"Because I find physical attraction less important than certain other qualities of heart and head, which are just those that Sara lacks, and which I recognize in you."

"It's a pity that I haven't a brother," she exclaimed, laughing.

Then, so that everything should be clear between us, I told her of my two conversations with Marchant. She became very serious again.

"Listen," she said, "you ought to talk over all this with your mother. If she is what I think her, she will understand you."

"Yes, I've been thinking so for a long time past, and I've made up my mind to speak to her one of these days—in a little while. But I shan't tell her what I have just told you about Dr. Marchant."

"Why not?"

"I think it's best not."

A kind of instinct warned me.

It was in October 1916 at Châtellerault, where I went to see my mother shortly before her death, that I was able to have the conversation with her that I had so long been planning. As I have said in the few words of preface to my mother's journal, which appeared under the name of *The School for Wives*, my mother had volunteered as nurse in a military hospital for contagious diseases, as dangerous in its way as the most exposed stations at the front. I had at first wanted to go with her; she had refused to let me. But she allowed me to pass a few days with her between two periods of ambulance service to which I had devoted myself. When I saw her again, she was in the nurse's costume which she never left. The hospital was full of patients; for fear of infection my mother would not let me go inside. And as I protested that she went in:

"Yes," she answered, laughing, "but we nurses are immune. Just think! After five months . . ."

This took place, as I have said, very few days before her death. I thought she looked tired out and overworked with day and night nursing; but when I told her she ought to take a little rest, she protested that she had never been better than since she had had no time to think of herself. And it was the same with the soldiers. "And with you too, I am sure," she added.

It is certain that I was feeling very much better now that I was entirely occupied with seeing to the transport of the wounded. My old troubles and anxieties seemed to have sunk into the background. I never thought of them, or only to give them a smile, and it was with perfect coolness that I began to speak to my mother about Dr. Marchant.

"I should like to know what you think of him," I said.

"I think he's one of our very best doctors, and, what's more, an excellent man."

"Yes, that's what everyone says. I should like a rather more personal opinion."

She sat silent for a long time, her eyes on the ground and a smile on her face. We were in the public gardens. It was a very fine day, and in spite of the lateness of the season the air was almost warm. Near us some pigeons, which had been picking up crumbs of bread thrown them by a passer-by, took flight. She looked at me, smiling still more and unable quite to control the slight tension of her features.

"Did you ever suspect," she began at last with a little tremble in her voice, "that I was in love with Dr. Marchant? For a mother to confess such a thing to her daughter is no doubt very—" She could not find a word to finish her sentence and went on: "It's a little secret I have never told anyone; and I should never have told you if I had anything to be ashamed of. A secret of no consequence, since I never tried to make him love me. But when I stopped caring for your father's esteem—that is to say, when I stopped esteeming him myself (I don't think this is news to you)—well, I had need of Dr. Marchant's esteem, and it's that that supported me during many sad and difficult moments."

"So you never told him? Why not?" (She shook her head but did not answer my "Why not?") "Are you sure he never suspected anything?"

She again remained silent for a few moments. Then:

"There was someone, though, who suspected something—his wife."

"Madame Marchant?"

"Yes; my friend. And it was because of her that I never said anything. I didn't want to make her suffer."

"Does she know at any rate of your sacrifice?"

"But, Geneviève, there was no sacrifice. It was better so."

"And are you sure that *he* never suspected anything?" I asked again a little impatiently.

She stopped smiling.

"Hardly anything."

Then she kissed me and, smiling once more, made a gesture with her hand as though to wave away these memories.

"Why am I telling you all this today, darling? Does it surprise you? Do you remember you once took it into your head (I really don't know why) that I was in love with poor dear Bourgweilsdorf?"

"Yes. It was ridiculous, but I had need to believe you loved someone who wasn't Father."

"Hush!" said she, as though gently scolding me. "You said dreadful things to me that day."

"I can only remember I was furious because I thought you were sacrificing yourself for me."

"And even if it had been so, Geneviève?" she said with extraordinary gravity.

"I abominate sacrifices."

"You talk like a person who has never yet loved. Let's walk a little, I'm rather cold. And it's nearly time for me to go back to the hospital."

A slight wind was beginning to rise and a few dead leaves fell to the ground.

We got up.

"I've something to tell you," I said, urged by a

sudden determination. And then all in a breath: "Do you know what I said to Dr. Marchant one day? That I wanted to have a child by him."

I saw her recoil a step or two, as if from a blow.

"Oh, Geneviève!" she exclaimed in a tone of voice impossible to define—shocked, but in an odd way that seemed a tiny bit feigned, disturbed too, and even a tiny bit amused. "I don't understand you," she added with trembling lips.

"Yes," I repeated brutally, "that I wanted him to make me the mother of a child."

"What possessed you, my poor darling?" and this time it was reproach that predominated in her voice.

"I don't know. Just an idea I had."

"And—what did he answer?" This time it was anxiety.

"He said I was talking like a child—a mad, indecent child; that he refused to take me seriously, that—"

"What else?"

"Well, he wouldn't because—"

"Because what? Come, don't be afraid."

"Because he loved his wife. But I understand to-day," I added, looking at her earnestly, "that it wasn't only because of that."

"Perhaps," she said in a whisper.

I thought her lips trembled. Oh, how much more admirable, above all how much more genuine, than my own egotistical resolutions seemed to me at that moment the delicate, uncommunicated feelings of my mother, of Dr. Marchant, and even of my aunt—all those mysterious and fragile threads woven secretly between heart and heart, which I had so roughly brushed through in my heedless, inconsiderate path. This is what I should have liked to say to her before we parted. But she put her finger, not on her own lips, but on mine, smiling tenderly and with a look that made me understand that there was no need of further words between us. Then I took her in my arms and embraced her with all my might. She bade me good-by.

I was never to see her again.